The Seasiders

The Seasiders

Skeletons in the Cupboard Series Book 2

A.J. Griffiths-Jones

For Dave

Author's Note

The characters in this novel are purely fictional. Any resemblance to people either alive or dead is pure coincidence, although it does contain a little of all of us. The location is fictional too; a town brought to life by my imagination set in 1960's England when a trip to the seaside was the highlight of every child's summer, mine included.

I have dedicated this work to my wonderful husband, who once again has been my backbone and given much needed constructive criticism throughout 'The Seasiders' creation. Although not an avid reader himself, Dave inspires my passion for writing by relentlessly supporting me to the full.

The beautiful cover design was painted by my very talented aunt, Sylvia Caswell, who continues to give me love and wisdom in everything that I do. Thanks also to Antony Caswell for his technical expertise in formatting the image.

A special mention goes to my great friend Jason McNeill, who has encouraged me through every twist and turn, and taken every step of this great adventure with me. Your encouragement has been second to none and I appreciate it. Although, watch out, you might find yourself in my next book!

The team at Creativia, especially Miika Hannila, have been fantastic throughout. They are professional and profound, taking marketing to new levels and giving their authors the much needed time and space to do what they do best, which is to write.

Thank you to everyone who read my first novel, 'The Villagers', and I sincerely hope that you enjoy the second in this series just as much. A lot of love and thought has been put into creating the characters, and although they never really existed, I do hope that they will capture a piece of your hearts.

Contents

Prologue

Who doesn't have fond memories of childhood trips to the seaside?

At some point in our lives, we have all been there, whether it was a busy Welsh coastal town with fun fairs and candy floss, a Northern resort with bright lights illuminating the promenade and a shingle beach, or a sleepy harbour on the South coast, with cream teas and donkey rides. The seaside was a place where we would either go to for a day trip, packed into the back of our parents' cars alongside picnics and the family dog, or longer stays where we would be allowed extra pocket money to spend on souvenirs and handfuls of copper to waste in the penny arcade.

When you are young, and excited about visiting these holiday places, you never quite comprehend that people actually live there all year round. They will be there in the winter trying hard to make a living from selling ice-cream that people are too cold to eat, or travelling to the cities to sell the shellfish that is too abundant for the locals to consume by themselves. Some might desperately try to hone their other talents such as painting or poetry, in the hope that next year their income will be two-fold and enough to help them survive the bitter frost when nobody comes to visit, save the few avid walkers that seek fresh air and solitude.

As children, we wouldn't have given a second thought to the seasiders whom we left behind after our day trip or when our holiday had come to an end, but their lives continued just the same as it

1

always had. We would travel home, sun-kissed and exhausted from the salty sea air, back to our homes, our families and our secrets. And just as we were bound to keep hidden gems that we only told those in our inner circle of friends, those seasiders held secrets of their own. Maybe not as shocking or as bold as those of their counterparts in the cities and towns but, nevertheless, they were things that were kept behind closed doors, shuffled away to a place where everyday folk couldn't see or hear about them, secrets that belonged exclusively to the seasiders. This is the tale of one such place.

Chapter One

Amazing Grace

Grace Thomas was in the middle of ironing a pile of white cotton table-cloths when she heard a loud bang, followed by the rantings of some-one cursing, coming from the garden. She carefully put down the iron and, leaning forward, pressed her nose against the cold window-pane to see where the noises had come from. As it happened it was nothing. Well, nothing out of the ordinary anyway.

Grace's husband, Dick, had been attempting to lay yet another slab on the patio but had lost his grip and the heavy concrete block had toppled to the ground, smashing into several chunks as it landed. Dick wasn't hurt, it looked as though only his ego was damaged, and he stood gazing at the broken slab in front of him with a very glum look on his face.

"Bloody fool', Grace muttered to herself as she turned back to her work, "That man should win an award for being the world's slowest worker!"

She wondered if she would ever be able to serve meals outside in the good weather, at this rate it seemed very unlikely. If only I had mar-ried a rich man, Grace mused. Although, the only remotely rich man in their town had been Rhys Pugh, and he'd moved away years ago. She looked around the kitchen and shrugged. Most of the appliances were in good condition, although they had all been handed down from either her or Dick's parents. The walls certainly needed a fresh coat of paint but there was no urgency and the floor tiles gleamed due to rigorous polishing. Life could have been a lot worse, Grace was well aware of that, but in the winter months when the guests were few and far between, her home was always just a little too silent.

Grace's thoughts were no reflection on the love that she felt for her husband, but simply a matter of truth. You see, Dick had been laying the patio for over twelve months, tediously raking the ground, laying a slab, repositioning the same piece of concrete and then needing to rest for five days before starting the process all over again. He claimed to have a bad back but Grace thought it was a disease called 'Lazyitis'. Her mother had warned her that all men suffered from it, especially when there were important jobs to be done around the house. But Dick was affectionate enough, in his own simple way. He always gave Grace a peck on the cheek before they went to sleep at night, never had to be asked to take the rubbish out and occasionally would buy her a small box of chocolates, just to show that he cared.

The Thomas's ran a guest house overlooking the seafront, well, if truth be told, Grace did so with very little help from Dick. He sometimes offered to help the guests to check out, and occasionally managed to repair a leaking tap or broken skirting board, but it was his wife who saw to most of the day to day running of the business. She would never admit it in public, but Grace liked to be in full control. The couple had inherited the establishment from Grace's parents some ten years before and, being brought up in its rooms, she found the day to day running both enjoyable and rewarding. The property stood just a few paces up a cliff road. White and detached, with ivy growing around the door, it looked very grand to the visitors as they approached. Three of the front windows faced the beach below and these were what Grace called her 'best rooms'. Spacious and immaculate, with comfy double beds, no better accommodation could be found in the town below, therefore from Easter to Halloween, the Thomas's made a good living from the business bestowed upon them. Grace had taken to it like a duck to water. It was just a pity that Dick felt like a duck too, but one very much out of the pond and his invisible wings flapped helplessly as he tried to keep up with his wife's demands. It was a bone of contention that Grace was left to see to almost everything. Over time she became annoyed that Dick seemed to disappear every time the telephone in the hallway rang. Grace didn't understand what was so difficult about making a booking. A large leather-bound ledger sat on the hall table, with lines drawn vertically upon the pages to clearly show which rooms were booked and which were vacant on any particular day. Nevertheless, there only had to be one tinkle and Dick would either take himself rapidly off in the opposite direction, or feign sleep if he happened to be in his chair. Grace knew that Dick had no problem talking to strangers, he would always have something polite or interesting to say to their guests, and he wrote with an impeccable cursive hand, so she really couldn't understand what was so difficult in writing down a few details in the bookings diary. Unless of course he was terrified of incurring his wife's wrath if he made a mistake, as he'd done once in the early days of their marriage. Yes, that was it, Grace supposed, she hadn't spoken to him for a week after Dick had stupidly reserved the same room for two different couples one summer. He obviously wanted to avoid a similar scenario.

For Dick's part, he thought Grace was amazing, but over the years had become oblivious to his own faults. He saw the patio project as a work in progress, with fine attention to detail being the order of the day. He was also unaware of his hours disappearing. Every morning he would lumber downstairs to eat his breakfast before a short walk to the newsagents. Dick wasn't allowed to have his paper delivered to the door, Grace only arranged that for 'paying guests' as she called them, besides her husband was always telling her that he liked a bit of sea breeze first thing. On returning from the shop, Dick would spend an hour in the softest armchair of their lounge, flicking through the pages at leisure. He would then spend another thirty minutes choosing which horses to bet on each afternoon. Dick Thomas was very proud of his ability to pick a winner, but even prouder of the fact that he could keep his hobby a closely guarded secret from his wife. You see, every afternoon Grace would write out a list of items that she needed Dick to fetch from the market or local store, and every afternoon her husband would amble off to buy them, with a slight detour to the betting shop.

So, quite understandably, by the time Dick had fetched the paper, read the paper, eaten breakfast and lunch, chosen his runners for the day, consumed six cups of tea and made his daily trip to the shops, he was too exhausted for anything else. Dick did get twinges in his back, the result of falling off his motorbike some years ago, but that wasn't the reason that the garden wasn't progressing as fast as his wife would have liked, it was simply a case of not being very good at it. He didn't mind the digging, the ground was soft enough, he just couldn't seem to get the hang of laying the slabs straight. Grace had very clearly told him that she wanted the patio finished for the summer. She just hadn't stated which summer.

Grace peeked outside again. Dick was still standing there, but now with one hand in his trouser pocket and the other mopping his brow with a giant handkerchief, as though he were waiting for someone to come along and help him clear up the mess. She did still love him, after all they'd been together over twenty years, but how things had changed. Gone was the suave and sophisticated young man freshly returned from the war, with his flashy smile and greased back hair, who used to take her out on his shiny red motorcycle. She saw hardly anything of that young man in her husband. Nowadays Dick was almost completely bald, overweight, and always tired. He didn't have a full day's work in him and Grace often wondered how a person who did so little could spend so much time either in bed or asleep in his armchair. Still, Dick was kind and had never even raised his voice to her, so she let him be.

Grace had kept her youthful figure, not least due to the number of times she had to run up and down the long flight of stairs every day. She also had her hair set every Thursday, ready for the new group of guests who would arrive on a Friday, for either a long weekend break or a proper beach holiday. Her hair hadn't changed in style for over a decade, Dick said he liked it that way, and so Grace stuck to having it put in rollers and generously laced with hairspray to hold it in place.

Grace liked to look her best and, every night before turning in, she would always carefully pick out her outfits for the next day. She loved her A-Line skirts and sensible trousers, matching them with patterned blouses with big frilly bows. Much younger girls, down in the town, were now starting to wear their skirts shorter but Grace was far too prim to follow fashion. She was a great lover of tweed and believed that a good jacket could transform even the dowdiest of outfits. Not that she got many chances to go out, of course. There were always sheets to change, bathrooms to scrub and food to cook. Still, she wouldn't have it any other way.

The couple hadn't been blessed with children, so all that they had were each other and their small circle of friends. Grace would have been happy to adopt, but Dick was more concerned about wagging tongues and genetic defects than giving an orphan a loving home. Therefore, time had passed and they now considered themselves too old, though both only just touching forty, and the likelihood of parenting was quickly fading away. Grace was an only child, so there was no chance of her becoming an aunt within her own family either, although Dick's siblings were many and produced a new set of nephews and nieces for them to dote on almost every year. Grace still had her parents to love and care for although, since their retirement some years ago, they did seem to spend more and more time travelling around, visiting stately homes and country teashops. They had refused to have a telephone installed, arguing that they were 'just up the road' but Grace had often walked the mile or so to their new bungalow only to find a note on the back door saying 'Gone out for the day' or 'Back at six, playing bridge with the Neath's'. Years ago, on the odd cold day when her parent's hadn't felt like venturing far, Grace would come down from her cleaning upstairs to find them both in the kitchen making a brew, smiling as if they still lived there and she was the guest. Grace loved those moments, especially as her mother always brought freshly baked fruit cake or a bread and butter pudding with her, which could be served to the guests as a treat after their evening meal.

The Thomas's family, friends and neighbours had been very kind, willing to lend a sympathetic ear in the early days of their marriage and careful not to broach the subject of 'little ones' in their later years. Grace still held out hope that a miracle might happen and that she would conceive naturally, but seeing as how she was always busy and Dick was always tired, the chance of them actually getting 'down to it' became more and more unlikely as the weeks and months passed. There was also the little matter of Dick's sleep-walking, which meant that Grace would often wake up alone in the middle of the night, venture downstairs and find him sitting in the kitchen or pottering about in his shed making invisible shelves or potting unseen plants. Maybe that's why he's always so tired in the day, Grace had thought, and that had been her sole reason for not nagging at him.

They didn't have much in common these days. Dick liked to listen to jazz, whereas Grace preferred the new music of Elvis Presley. It did no harm that the young singer was handsome too. Dick rarely picked up a book, whilst Grace could easily have immersed herself in a library and never surfaced in the outside world again. On the rare winter days that the couple found themselves with no guests and nothing to do, Dick would suggest inviting friends for a drink and a bite to eat while Grace, simply nodding her head and relenting, wished dearly that they could go for a walk or have a romantic meal alone in one of the two restaurants that opened for a few hours in the dark months.

Despite, feeling that life was passing her by far too quickly, Grace was content with her lot. She certainly held no secrets, like some folk she could mention. The Thomas's weren't gossips by any stretch of the imagination but during their years as proprietors of the 'Sandybank Guest House', the couple had learned that there were all kinds of goings on amongst the residents below. Their elevated position, high above the town, had given Dick and Grace a bird's-eye view of some of the trysts and affairs that went on, and for that which they didn't see with their own eyes, the electric dryer in Maureen O'Sullivan's hair salon had provided an excellent location to learn the rest. Grace looked forward to Thursdays more than any other day of the week.

It was like having the plot of a book unfold before her eyes when the gossipmongers were in the right mood, and besides, she liked having her hair done too.

As Grace carried the finished tablecloths through to the dining room, she wondered if she had time to spend half an hour with a book and a cup of tea before she needed to start preparing dinner for her guests. It was still early in the season and only two of the six rooms were occupied, both by elderly gentlemen, no doubt staying for some fresh air and long walks, Grace presumed. Most families who came to the area chose one of the cheaper holiday options and either rented a chalet on the site just out of town, where both entertainment and food were included in the price, or they hired a static caravan for their stay and made the short walk to the seaside down steps from the cliff top above. Therefore, it was mostly couples and singles who paid to be pampered at the 'Sandybank' and once word had got out about the soft feather mattresses and Grace's excellent cooking skills, the ledger was littered with bookings from season start to season end. There would be nothing fancy tonight, just a slice of gammon with an egg and new potatoes so, as it wouldn't take her long, she might even boil up some cabbage to go on the side. Albeit a simple meal, the little tables would still be set with shiny silver cutlery, china plates and little matching cruet sets that Grace had proudly purchased from a new department store on one of her rare trips out to the next town. Tiny glass vases held a few spring flowers and napkins were folded into fans, nothing was too good for the Thomas's guests.

After seeing that her dining room was perfect for the two gentlemen to sit down and eat, Grace peered through the serving hatch dividing that room from the kitchen. Still no sign of Dick, he must be nursing his pride in the garden, she thought. Gently putting her hand through to the kitchen worktop, she placed her palm on the teapot, it was still warm. Grace pushed open the door and sat down at the kitchen counter. Slipping her Mary Jane's off her feet, Grace wriggled her toes and picked up her Mills and Boone romance novel from the Welsh dresser. She glanced up at the orange plastic clock ticking away above the stove, it was four o'clock. Plenty of time for an hour of literary indulgence before her guests would be back from their various pursuits and expecting a pot of tea, and just enough time to see if the heroine, Catherine, could catch her handsome beau. Very soon Grace was whisked away to a time of Victorian courtship and elegant ballgowns. It was far, far away from her current life, in a small seaside town, in 1964.

Chapter Two

Maureen O'Sullivan

It was Thursday. For Grace, this was the most important day of the week as, at 11am sharp, she would set off down the hill to the hairdressing salon in town where, for an hour and a half, she could forget about the guest house, drink Camp coffee with frothy milk and catch up on the weekly gossip. It had been fairly ordinary morning so far, with only one guest to cook breakfast for but, as was her habit, Grace still bustled around tidying and plumping.

"Are you sure you won't have another cup of tea Mr. Brown?" she urged, teapot poised, fussing around the lone gentleman sitting stiffly at the smallest table.

"Not for me, thank you Mrs. Thomas", the old man replied, gently placing a hand over the top of his empty teacup, "I have a long journey home, so I should go and pack my suitcase."

"I do hope you've enjoyed your stay", Grace smiled "Was everything to your satisfaction?"

"Of course, excellent as usual", the man nodded, folding up the newspaper and then looking up at his host, "You run a top notch guest house Mrs. Thomas."

Grace glowed with pride. "So, we'll see you again in September as usual Mr. Brown?"

"No doubt you will", her guest replied, rising from his seat and heading towards the door, "I'll give you a call when I'm in need of another break."

Grace followed him out to the foot of the stairs where he had already started the ascent to his room, needing to get his belongings together and check out. She watched him place his well-manicured right hand on the rail as he moved silently upwards. Mr. Brown had the appearance of an old history professor, with his neat tweed trousers and burgundy bow tie, someone incredibly intelligent and prone to doing a lot of thinking. Grace had never pried, she never asked any of her guests what they did for a living, but most of them volunteered the information at some time or another. Although, a regular for three years now, Mr. Brown had never given away any personal details, but Grace didn't mind, besides it was fun trying to guess how he made his money, back home in the city. She continued to watch the genteel man, noting that his hair was so neat that he must have recently had it cut. His back was arched a little as though he carried a heavy burden. That must be from years of stooping over his desk, Grace thought. Suddenly her guest stopped and turned towards her.

"I say, would you mind awfully if I check out an hour later Mrs. Thomas? Seeing as I'm the only guest. I'd quite like to pop down to the front for some toffee and scones to take home."

Grace stopped smiling and gritted her teeth. A late check-out! It was unheard of at the Sandybank. She had very clearly stated in the guest rules that rooms must be vacated by 10am. It was her routine, and she couldn't have her routine disrupted. She liked to open the windows, strip the sheets off the beds and put them into her new automatic twin-tub before heading for her hair appointment. Any delay would mean she would be late with her other tasks and everything would be out of sync. Grace took a breath and looked up into Mr. Brown's watery blue eyes.

"Of course, no problem at all", she told him, "Take your time, there's absolutely no rush."

The gentleman smiled briefly and then headed on up to his room, leaving Grace alone to panic.

She immediately pushed open the door to the dining room and started collecting up the dirty crockery, clattering the cup and saucer, and cursing as she did so. Grace pushed everything through the little hatch that connected to the kitchen and felt the heat rising on her neck. She leaned forward to look at the clock, it was 9am. If Mr. Brown intended to check out an hour late, that would be eleven. From past experience, Grace knew that it would be a palaver, as this particular guest always insisted on checking his bill carefully, counting out his money twice just in case any notes were stuck together and then would want a written invoice which he would read slowly before finally departing. All of this would mean that she would be late for her hair appointment, late washing the sheets and late, just late with everything.

Grace entered the kitchen feeling ready to throw something. Luckily, Dick was standing there, patiently waiting for the kettle to boil. Grace looked down at the grubby fingernails that her husband was tapping on the work surface and fought the urge to yell. My goodness, Dick was really letting himself go, she fumed. You only had to look at Mr. Brown's immaculate nails to know that he was a proper gentleman.

"You've got a face like thunder woman, whatever is the matter?" Dick asked, trying to look sincere.

"Mr. Brown wants to check out at eleven instead of ten", Grace huffed, "And it's my hair day."

"So", muttered Dick, not quite understanding what all the fuss was about, "I'll check him out."

"It's not just that, is it?" moaned his wife, "What about the sheets and everything?"

"I'm pretty sure I can manage to pull a couple of sheets off the bed", replied Dick, leaning across the counter to see what he could find in the biscuit tin, "And if you show me how to set the washer, I'll put them in for you as well."

Grace stopped in her tracks and stared at her husband. It was very unlike Dick to help with what he called 'women's chores'. Still, she didn't intend to miss her shampoo and set, so she stepped forward and planted a kiss on her husband's cheek.

"Thank you love, that would be wonderful."

Dick rolled his eyes and tutted, "I'm not completely useless you know."

His words fell on deaf ears, as Grace had already turned away and started running water in the sink to wash the dishes. She hummed a little tune as the bubbles rose and everything was back to normal.

Dick finished making his cup of tea and, gathering up the handful of biscuits that he'd selected from the tin, wandered outside towards his potting shed. An hour with his newspaper was just what he needed.

By eleven o'clock Grace had hoovered the dining room with her upright vacuum, spluttered over the dust collected in the bag as she emptied it into the dustbin and dried all the plates and cups from the draining board. Taking off her apron, she smoothed down her long-sleeved orange flowery dress and looked in the mirror. A smattering of lipstick and a silk headscarf and she would be ready to go.

"Dick, I'm going now", she called as she struggled into her coat, "Don't forget about the sheets. I've written the instructions down on how to set the machine."

A weary head peered around the kitchen door and nodded, "No problem love."

"And make sure you make him another pot of tea before he leaves," Grace added sternly, "The pot is ready on the side just there." She indicated towards the tray on the side with her forefinger.

So, satisfied that Mr. Brown and the dirty sheets were in fairly capable hands, Grace slipped out of the back door and headed down the road towards the seafront.

Being the last week in March, it was a blustery morning and Grace pushed her hands deep into her coat pockets to keep them warm. It had been a quiet few months but Easter was just around the corner, and that would signify the start of the holiday season. As she strolled downhill, Grace could see the local fishermen repairing their boats and diligently checking the nets. She often wondered what it would be like to spend the night out at sea, she imagined it to be peaceful and calm, with only the sounds of the waves to lull you to sleep. There certainly wouldn't be the likes of Dick snoring out there. Grace had spent a fitful six hours tossing and turning the night before, as her husband snored like a bear, oblivious to his own volume levels. Grace thought it a good job that their bedroom was on the opposite side of the house to their guests, she would have died of embarrassment had they ever complained about the noise.

As Grace turned the corner, Maureen O'Sullivan's salon came into view. The outer window-frame was painted a vivid shade of pink and had the words 'Maureen's Hair' stuck onto the glass. It looked bright and trendy, a lovely place to relax and unwind. There were several seagulls strutting around on the pavement outside the salon door and Grace shooed them away with her handbag before entering. The inside of the hairdressing salon was just as inviting and colourful as the outside, with turquoise and cream wallpaper, large posters depicting various hairstyle trends and a pink transistor radio blaring out the sounds of Bobby Vinton, Chubby Checker and Brenda Lee.

Grace liked coming here on Thursdays, as it was the only day that Maureen worked alone, with her assistant, Patsy, having the day off. Grace didn't know much about the hairdresser's personal life, except that she was divorced, had a teenage son and knew everything there was to know about the people in the town around her. Seeing as Grace was married and had no children, it was the latter point that made coming to the salon the highlight of her week. She wouldn't describe herself as being a nosey parker, but it was always nice to know what people were up to, seeing as she was up the hill, out of the hub of everyday life. Well, that's what Grace liked to tell herself anyway!

"Morning Grace, be with you in a minute love," shouted Maureen from the back room, quickly stubbing out her cigarette and giving her hands a quick rinse in the sink.

"No hurry," Grace smiled, carefully removing her headscarf and coat. She looked at herself sideways in the vanity mirror and sighed. She looked even more windswept and flustered than usual.

"Now then," Maureen enthused, stepping in to view, "Same as usual today, or do you fancy a drastic change? What about a Marilyn Monroe style to start the summer season?"

Grace giggled and shook her head, "Goodness me no! What would Dick say if I went home looking like a blonde bombshell?"

"He'd thank his lucky stars, I reckon", teased the hairdresser, "Best stick to your shampoo and set, we don't want him having a heart attack now do we?"

Grace shook her head and handed her belongings to the busty middle-aged woman who was waiting to get started, and helped herself to a nylon cape from the rack. She often wondered what it would be like to have Maureen's long curly hair and brightly coloured wardrobe. Today, the hairdresser had purposely clashed a deep purple blouse with a bold brown-patterned pinafore, and looked every bit the sixties diva. Her long brunette hair hung in ringlets down her back and a silky cream scarf was tied over the top and round to the nape of the woman's neck, making a very fashionable headband. Grace tried not to look too envious.

"Ooh, let's turn the music up a bit for this one", Maureen suddenly squealed, as Chubby Checker's popular 'Let's Twist Again' started playing, and she began swinging her hips back and forth in tune to the song.

"I haven't heard this one before", said Grace, listening intently, "Is he an American?"

Maureen giggled, "You need to get with it Grace, this is what all the youngsters are listening to."

"Well, we're hardly…" Grace began, suddenly catching herself. Maybe she was getting too old in her ways, she realised, Maureen was around the same age but acted and dressed much younger.

The start of the comment had been lost on the hairdresser, who considered herself far younger in attitude and outlook than most of her clients, and she continued to smile at Grace, waiting for her to continue.

"Oh, never mind," Grace sighed, "It is a catchy tune, isn't it?"

Just then, the little bell above the door tinkled and another seaside resident wandered in for her hair appointment. She was about seventy-five years old and wore a sensible camel coat and fuzzy brown fur hat. Grace recognised her immediately as the lady who owned the sweet shop and waved across at her.

"Hello", she mouthed, "Nice to see you Mrs. Cole."

"Take a seat Mrs. Cole," yelled Maureen, taking the old lady's progressing deafness in to consideration, "You're very early today love, I need to see to Grace first."

The pensioner raised her hand slightly and headed for a chair in the corner of the room where she promptly began looking through the adverts in the local gazette.

"So, what's new up at the big house then?" asked Maureen O'Sullivan as she helped Grace to gently ease herself into a comfortable position, with her head tipped back over the sink.

"Ooh, it's very quiet this week Mo," Grace sniffed, "But we've got lots booked in for Easter."

"That's good," smiled the hairdresser, pumping shampoo into her hand from a liquid dispenser, "Now are you sure you wouldn't like a change this week?"

Grace looked forlornly at the other woman's sleek mane, what she'd give to walk out of the salon with those perfect curls cascading down her back. Gently she shrugged and replied in the negative, there wasn't much point in changing her hair, she sighed, nobody noticed anyway.

"Any news in town?" asked Grace, tentatively changing the subject.

"Now you come to mention it, yes!" Maureen gasped, and she filled Grace in on the comings and goings of certain residents as she alternately massaged and rinsed her client's hair.

Meanwhile, back at the Sandybank Guest House, Dick had been busy choosing his runners for the day. There were only a few races that afternoon, and he was carefully deciding whether to put his wa-ger all on one horse or to distribute the cash in small amounts over each of the three races. Decisions such as these were of considerable importance to Dick as he rarely found enjoyment in other hobbies and had learned quite early on that he could win a small fortune by carefully studying the form.

So engrossed in his task was he that it was a little after twelve o'clock when Dick remembered his promise about the bedsheets. It hadn't taken as long as he'd expected to sort out Mr. Brown and with both his armchair and cup of coffee still warm, Dick had been tempted to sit back down instead of attending to the guest room. As a result, looking up at the clock in horror, he was now all too aware that he needed to move like lightning in order to start the sheets on their cy-cle before his dear wife returned home.

Gently pushing his newspaper to one side, Dick got to his feet and opened the sitting room door. It shouldn't take long to pull a couple of sheets off the bed, but he knew only too well that Grace would bend his ear about the linens not being finished and on the washing-line. Smiling to himself, Dick shrugged, just another excuse for her to have a good moan he thought, as he heaved his cumbersome body upstairs to begin the thankless chore of stripping Mr. Brown's vacant room.

Grace closed her eyes and winced slightly as Maureen O'Sullivan wound the curlers tightly to her client's head. Gosh, that didn't half hurt sometimes she pondered, but the hairdresser had insisted that if she set the rows too loosely, Grace's hair would be all over the place by a Sunday morning. So, instead of complaining, Grace opened a back-copy of Woman's Weekly focusing particular interest on the knitting patterns and recipes. Sometimes, when the salon proprietor wasn't looking, Grace would gently tear out a page that featured a new way with meat or fish. There was nothing she liked more than to impress her guests with a few new culinary delights. Some time later, Grace was gently disturbed from her reading by Maureen's perfect red nails patting her shoulder.

"Time for the dryer sweetheart," purred the hairdresser, "I'll pop you under for twenty minutes."

Grace dutifully rose from her chair, her knees giving a faint crack as she stretched, and padded over to the row of upright hairdryers that lined the wall opposite the door. She sat down, waiting for Maureen to adjust the hood to the required height and couldn't help gazing wistfully at the wonderful head of hair at her side. Lucky woman, thought Grace, Maureen knows how attractive that hair of hers makes her look.

Suddenly there was a loud pop.

"Dammit," cursed the hairdresser, 'Bloody thing's stuck, oops, excuse my language Grace."

Grace smiled, "No problem Mo, can I do anything to help?"

"Would you mind just moving out from under it?" Maureen huffed, 'Just for a minute."

Grace pulled herself to her feet for the third time that morning and waited patiently while her friend twiddled with the adjuster at the back of the dryer.

"What on earth is stopping it from going down?" panted Maureen, now sticking her head up underneath the little plastic hood, "I can't get the damned thing to move."

With that, she gave an almighty shove and the machine snapped down into position. Maureen gave a sigh of relief and proceeded to pull her head out from underneath the hood.

However, the brunette had failed to realise that her silky headscarf had caught on the knob inside and when Maureen started to pull her head back out, something important was left behind. That important item being her beautiful long hair!

Grace gave an involuntary squeal as her, now bald, friend desperately tried to unhook her wig from inside the dryer. This was the very last thing the guest house owner had expected to see!

Poor Maureen managed to free her precious curls within seconds, but to her client it seemed that time had stood still as she took in the unbelievable sight in front of her.

"Please...sit..." stammered the hairdresser, pointing helplessly at the seat as she dashed in to the back room, the wig dangling from her fingers, "I'll be....back in a......"

Grace politely dropped her gaze to the floor and did as she was instructed. She had absolutely no idea what to say, even if the words had formed themselves on her lips she would still have been dumbstruck.

Not knowing quite what to do either, Grace turned the huge black timer to the number twenty and sat back, waiting for her hair to dry. For a split second, she had considered leaving Maureen to deal with her misfortune in private but going out into the main street, with a head full of curlers, was not an option that Grace Thomas was willing to consider. She glanced over to Mrs. Cole in the corner, but the old lady was fast asleep in her chair. It would be just as well to stay put.

After another nineteen minutes of sitting under the warm air, wondering what she should say or do, Grace felt the timer ping and heard the familiar clicking of Maureen's heels on the tiled floor coming towards her. She slowly peeked out from under the dryer. The hairdresser was once again resplendent in her wig and acted as though nothing had happened.

"Time to take out your curlers," she smiled, "Won't take long and we'll have you all ready for home." Grace searched her friend's eyes for a hint of upset or embarrassment but there was only a knowing twinkle, holding the knowledge that her kind friend Grace would tell no-one about what she had seen.

While events were unfolding at the hair salon, Dick had let himself into the single guest bedroom half way down the long corridor.

Painted in a cool and calming tone of duck-egg blue, with an elegant quilted white eiderdown gracing the bed, this was Mr. Brown's preferred room and Grace always made sure that she kept it free on this particular week of the year for him. There was little evidence that anyone had slept in the room at all, save a little rumpling of the pillows, Dick noticed. It seemed that Mr. Brown was as tidy in his habits as he was in his apparel. There was no litter in the wicker waste paper basket and no sign of any stray hairs on the bedcovers. In fact, the room looked almost as spotless as when their guest had arrived.

Dick wondered, just for a second or two, whether he could get away with pretending to have already washed and dried the sheets. But then he thought better of trying to trick his wife, it wasn't even twelve-thirty yet and she well knew that the laundry took a good two hours to dry on the line, even on a very windy day like today. Besides, the big give away would be that he'd actually put the darn things back on the bed, something that Dick had never done in all their years as guest house proprietors. And so, gently tugging off the top layer, Dick deposited the pillows at the foot of the bed and began pulling off the sheets.

Suddenly, as he whisked the bottom sheet towards him, Dick heard a little plop on the floor beside his feet. He looked down and saw that a small book had dropped out from under the mattress. He stooped down, with some degree of difficulty, and picked it up. The cover was pale cream with orange lettering, and depicted the sketch of a kangaroo.

"All This And Bevin Too", Dick read aloud, his words echoing off the high ceiling.

He turned the book over. It certainly didn't look very interesting. The author had a strange name too.

"Quentin Crisp", he said slowly, feigning an upper-class accent and sticking his nose in the air.

Dick gathered up the sheets and headed back downstairs, with the paperback tucked securely in the pocket of his cardigan. Grace is always nagging at me about broadening my mind, he thought, so I'll read this book, just to show her that I'm not totally stupid. But not today though, he didn't have time for sitting about with his head in a book today. Just then the phone rang which, after briefly glaring at it for a few seconds, Dick ignored.

Back at the salon, Grace had paid Maureen for her services and made another appointment for the same time on the following week. Despite a mild horror at her earlier discovery, Grace felt that she had a duty to support her friend's business. Besides, even if she had felt too awkward to return, Maureen's Salon was the only one of its kind in the town. She really couldn't afford the time, or extra expense, of travelling elsewhere for her shampoo and set. As she tied her headscarf securely under her chin, to protect her perfectly set hair from the wind outside, Grace glanced over at Maureen O'Sullivan, who was now frantically brushing old Mrs. Coles' silver grey hair. Apart from the salon owner's locks being slightly cockeyed on her head, she appeared, by all intents, to be perfectly fine. Grace left feeling a sense of relief.

Stepping outside, Grace was tempted to pause briefly to look in the bookshop window. She liked nothing more than a good romance novel, and was delighted to see that several new ones were now fanned out on a shiny red cloth in front on her. Pausing for a second or two to check the money in her purse, Grace slid inside and began to peruse the shelves. The book covers looked very enticing. Dreamy women and shirtless men gazed forlornly into each other's eyes, their lips puckered for that first magical kiss, with a golden sunset behind them in the perfect paradise location. Grace bit her lip as she selected one from the shelf. The background depicted a country manor with acres of sprawling green fields and a perfectly blue sky. On the steps of the house stood a beautiful young woman in Edwardian dress, gazing lovingly at the man in the foreground, who looked more like a stable hand than a gent. It was so obviously a love that was never meant to be. This is the one, thought Grace, forbidden love will make for a great read.

The pavement on the opposite side of the hairdresser's curved round a bend to the left, so that any pedestrians walking on that side could take in the full panoramic views of the beach and the waves lapping on the shore. It was in this direction that Grace now found herself walking slowly home.

"Aye aye there, Mrs. Thomas," a male voice called, "Will you be needing any fish this week?"

Grace turned sharply to see the rugged face of a local fisherman trotting up behind her, his boots still covered in fish guts and seaweed from the morning's catch. She liked Robbie Powell. Although a good decade younger than the Thomas's, he was a very polite young man and always found the time to stop for a chat. Robbie was now taking long strides to catch up with Grace, causing his thick black curls to bob up and down as he walked.

"What? Oh, sorry Robbie," Grace flushed, her cheeks turning pink, "I didn't realise it was you."

"Why's that then?" joked the fisherman, wiping his damp fingers on his dungarees, "Have you been getting your fish elsewhere?"

"No," Grace responded sharply, "Look, I'm really sorry, it's been a very strange morning."

The fisherman stopped in his tracks and smiled. "I'm only joking love, it's fine. Are you okay, Mrs. Thomas? I hope nobody's been up-setting you."

Grace felt the heat rising in her cheeks again and told herself she was acting like a fool.

"I'll tell you what," she began, thinking quickly, "I've got a house full next weekend, what with Easter coming up, why don't you bring me some mackerel and prawns on Friday."

"Right you are," beamed Robbie, happy to be gaining some more custom, "I'll come up about ten."

Grace thanked the man and, as soon as he walked away, she looked out onto the beach. She could vaguely make out the silhouettes of a few locals walking their dogs on the sand and the shape of a dozen or more seagulls circling the cliff overhead in search of scraps. The town behind her was starting to get busier as the day went on, and a few vehicles were now making their way through the central street. Life always carries on as usual, she thought. No matter what changes had occurred between her and Maureen O'Sullivan, life, in general, was the same.

Grace vowed not to tell anyone about the incident that morning, not even Dick. No, especially not Dick. She could just imagine her husband telling all his friends about Mo's misfortune, as he tossed back a pint or two at the local tavern. Well, if anybody ever did find out what was under Maureen O'Sullivan's hair, it wouldn't come from her, Grace owed it to her friend to keep a confidence, and by God she would. Now, she sniffed, pulled herself together and started the steep walk up towards the Sandybank Guest House, It was at moments like these that she was very glad of her sensible shoes and warm tweed coat. Grace looked upwards to where her imposing white house stood. She was a very proud lady and strode up the cliff road full of purpose. Let's go and see what that lazy oaf of a husband is up to, she thought.

Dick had been very busy in his wife's absence. Not only had he stripped the bed as requested, and stuffed the sheets into the twin-tub, Grace's husband had also picked a bunch of daffodils from the border and placed them in a vase, and was now busy laying yet another concrete slab on top of his ever-expanding patio project. He had also managed to avoid answering the bright red Bakelite telephone, three times.

Grace didn't bother to see if Dick was in the back garden. No doubt he would be, she thought, as that was where he seemed to lurk at this hour every day. She was convinced that the purpose was to look busy, should Grace happen to open the kitchen window to inform him that lunch was ready. As she opened the back door Grace was immediately taken aback by the lack of noise. By her calculation, the sheets should still be twisting and twirling around in the tub, but they weren't. Grace turned to the machine in the corner and lifted the lid. Sheets were in, powder was in, but no water! She looked up at the socket on the wall. It was plugged in properly but the power switch was still in the 'OFF' position. A tiny bit of bile rose in her throat as Grace fought the urge to scream.

"Diiicccckkkk!!" she yelled, "You lazy, good-for-nothing, useless piece of…"

Dick had already heard the vibrations through the open kitchen window, as his wife gave vent to her frustration and sat huddled under the windowsill out of sight. His plan was to wait until Grace stomped off to another room and then make a hasty retreat down the path to the pub, where he fully intended to stay until her blood pressure had deflated a little. He cursed himself too. Why he couldn't follow out the simplest instructions was a complete mystery. But now, come to think of it, Grace had said nothing about flicking the switch on the wall, so how could he be fully to blame?

Dick waited fifteen minutes and then shuffled on all fours around the side of the house. He only needed to get past the kitchen door, with its one chest-height panel of glass, and then he'd be safe enough to get back up on his feet and head down the hill towards the pub. Therefore, taking a deep breath and slow careful movements, he maneuvered the path with ease, reaching the corner of the house just a few feet away from the back door. A foot away now, he stopped and listened. He couldn't hear Grace moving around inside, but unfortunately the washer was now grumbling away under its heavy load, so Dick found it impossible to tell if the coast was clear or not.

He listened intently. There were no pots and pans clattering around the kitchen. No cupboard doors being banged and no sound of heavy scrubbing or cleaning. There was nothing but silence. Grace must have gone into another room to think about next week's menu, Dick thought, torn between the idea of getting up or staying put and having forty winks. Deciding to make a run for it, the hefty man scrambled to his feet just in time to find the door being opened in front of him. As he stood up to his full height, Dick felt his newly found book tumble out of his pocket and on to the path at his feet.

"Well, well, what have we here?" Grace sneered, grabbing the paperback, "Going somewhere?"

"Erm, no dear," spluttered Dick, trying to think quickly, which was never an easy task for him.

"Good," replied his wife rather tersely, "I was just about to make us a sandwich."

"Smashing," smiled Dick, shocked by the mild manner in which Grace had greeted him.

"You can sit down and tell me all about your morning", Grace continued, smiling widely but masking a rising temper tantrum "I would love to hear all about your incompetence, laziness and countless cups of coffee." Strangely, Grace's clever sarcasm gave her a huge sense of pride.

Dick bowed his head and stretched out a hand to take the book from his wife's grasp.

"Oh no you don't!" she cried indignantly, "I'm going to hang on to this for a while."

"But it's just a book about a kangaroo..."

"Mmm, so it is," noticed Grace looking at the cover, "Here have it then, at least that will be one book that you've read in your lifetime."

With that, she thrust the little paperback into Dick's arms and inclined her head towards the kitchen table and chairs, where they usually took their meals.

"Sit," she ordered, tying an apron around her waist, "I want to hear all about your busy morning."

Chapter Three

Robbie Powell

It was Good Friday and Grace had spent a busy week spring-cleaning the guest house. Each room had been aired, floors given a wax polish and eiderdowns hung out on the washing-line to freshen them up. She'd been to her regular hair appointment the day before, albeit a bit cautiously, but as it turned out, Maureen was her usual cheerful self and readily filled Grace in on the town's gossip. There was no awkwardness between them and nothing was mentioned about the 'incident'.

Dick, being afraid of either getting in the way or getting told off, had spent most of his time avoiding going indoors. He much preferred to tidy the potting shed, pull weeds from the flower beds or disappear to the betting shop. There had been a few silent days after what he liked to refer to as the 'Sheet Saga' but now things were getting back to normal. Dick knew that Grace was in her element when the place was full of guests and the weekend's arrivals would be sure to put her in a good mood. He had glanced at the leather book in the hallway and had counted a family of four arriving this afternoon, two single gents tonight and two couples tomorrow morning. That would mean that the Sandybank was full to its capacity. It would also mean a healthy amount of money going into their bank account too.

Desperately in need of a cup of coffee to boost her energy levels, Grace sat in the kitchen looking wistfully at her latest romance book on the work surface. She'd have to wait until bedtime to finish this one, too much to do today, although it was a shame, as the plot was good and the characters feisty. How she loved being carried away to another realm by the power of books. Brushing her hand over the cover, Grace smiled. Look at that handsome brute, with his chiseled jaw and thick dark hair, she thought, men in real life just don't live up to those standards. She was disturbed from her daydreaming by Dick, who had opened the back door and was slowly wiping his muddy feet on the bristly mat outside the door.

"Any chance of a coffee for me?" he grinned cheekily at his wife, "I've been ever so busy."

Grace rolled her eyes and got up to make a drink for her husband.

"Oh yes, what's kept you occupied this morning then?" she asked, "Have you been reading again?"

Dick felt the verbal dig like a poke in the ribs. Grace knew he was struggling to read that little book he'd found the previous week, supposing that it was far too intellectual for his simple tastes. The truth was, he didn't really understand most of it, instead being much more intrigued by the author. It was the way in which he imagined other people to pronounce the name 'Quentin Crisp' that had stirred him to do a bit of careful investigation. Some of his mates at the pub had heard of the arty and eccentric Mr. Crisp and laughed when Dick had happened to mention that he was reading poetry by that very same gent. One chap in particular had commented that Dick would be wearing a silk cravat and fedora next time they saw him, but Dick didn't understand all the fuss. If he decided to suddenly smarten himself up it would be because he wanted to, not because of a book with a kangaroo on the front, he'd retorted.

"I've been weeding down the front path," he told Grace, "And I've cut back the hedges too."

Grace smiled, she shouldn't be hard on him today, not when he'd genuinely been doing some work.

Dick coughed. "Do you need me to get anything from town dear?" he casually asked, hoping for a chance to get away to place his bets and have a sneaky afternoon pint.

Grace thought for a moment and then suddenly lit up, as though she'd just had a major revelation.

"Thank goodness you asked," she grinned, "We'll need a couple of legs of lamb for Sunday."

"Bloody hell", choked Dick, spluttering coffee over his shirt, "Lamb! What's wrong with giving them chicken?" He blotted madly at his front with a damp tea towel.

"For goodness sake Dick, do we have to go through this every year?" gasped Grace, "It's Easter Sunday this weekend, and it's always been our tradition to serve lamb."

"Yes, and it costs a lot more too," grumbled her husband, "Twice the price of a bloody chicken."

"Just get it will you, I really don't have time to sit here arguing with you."

With that, Grace placed her cup in the sink, and moved towards the door.

"Oh, and change your shirt, you mucky pup," she tutted, "What will people think?"

Dick sipped the last of his coffee and looked down at the romance novel that his wife had left behind. He picked it up and read the story outline on the back cover.

"Brought together by mysterious circumstances, the lives of Margaret and Brett are turned upside down when they realise how deeply they feel for one another. Will the course of true love run smooth or does a close encounter with a stranger threaten to tear them apart?" he read silently to himself.

'What a load of old twaddle," Dick chuckled loudly, "None of that 'being struck by cupid's arrow' happens in real life. It's a quick courtship, get married, get nagged at for half a century and then keel over."

He shoved the book away and heaved himself off the stool on which he'd been sitting for the past ten minutes. Dick felt mildly happy now. At least having to go to the butcher's shop would give him a good excuse to attend to his own little tasks in town. If only Grace knew what he got up to half the time, he thought, shaking his head in disbelief, she'd have my guts for garters.

The trouble was, Grace knew exactly how her husband chose to spend his time.

As Dick struggled into his jacket there was a loud rap on the back door.

Opening it, he was greeted by the smiling face of Robbie Powell who, as promised, was holding a large basket of fresh seafood in his arms.

"Alright Dick," the lad chuckled, seeing Dick still entangled with the sleeve of his jacket, "Let me put this down and help you with that."

"Ah, thanks Robbie. Bloody thing's getting too small. I reckon Grace shrunk it in the wash."

Robbie laughed and kept his thoughts to himself. He hadn't seen Dick for a couple of weeks and was surprised to see that the older man's waistline had expanded quite significantly.

Just then, almost as if she had sensed her husband using her name in vain, Grace appeared through the other door. She was holding a battered leather purse in her hand.

"Hello Robbie love," she grinned, "Is that our fish for tonight's supper?"

Robbie nodded and placed the basket on the draining board, "It certainly is, Mrs. T."

Grace simultaneously counted out money to give to Dick to buy the lamb and paid the fisherman what she owed for the mackerel and prawns.

"Have you got time for a cuppa and a slice of walnut cake?" Grace offered kindly, knowing that Robbie had probably come straight up from his boat and wouldn't have stopped for a drink or a bite to eat yet.

"Aye, go on then." Robbie replied, rubbing his hands together. There was nothing he liked more than a big wedge of Mrs. Thomas's cake. She baked almost as well as his granny.

"Sit down then," she fussed, putting on the kettle and reaching for a tea plate on which to put the cake.

Dick could see that he wasn't needed and said his goodbyes, thankful that Robbie was there, thus avoiding any last minute sarcasm from his wife.

"So," the young man smiled, "What's on the agenda for this weekend then? Lots of guests, and lots of cooking to do?"

Grace replied in the affirmative and proceeded to tell Robbie all about the regular guests that would be staying this weekend and the new couple whom she knew nothing about except that they'd just got married and had chosen the Sandybank Guest House as their honeymoon location.

With the fish put away in the refrigerator, tea poured and walnut cake served, the conversation took an unexpected turn.

"So, what do you think will happen to Margaret and Brett?" Robbie asked, unexpectedly pulling Grace's Mills and Boone saga towards him.

"Gosh," was all Grace could say, quite taken aback by the young man's interest in her book.

"Do you think Stephen is a long lost relative or something?' Robbie continued, quite oblivious to the shocked look that Grace was giving him, "Or is he an ex-lover?"

"Well…" started Grace, suddenly realising that Robbie must have actually read this book to know so much about the characters, "I'm not sure."

Robbie looked a little disappointed at Grace's apparent lack of interest and pushed the novel away.

"I'm sorry," Grace apologised, "I just didn't think that would be the sort of thing that young men read."

"I'm full of surprises," Robbie winked cheekily, "And I love these romantic sagas I do."

And so, for another half hour, Robbie and Grace discussed the plot and characters, other books that they'd both read by the same author and how lovely it was to get away from real life sometimes.

All of a sudden, the telephone rang, interrupting their chatter. Grace excused herself and walked into the hallway to answer it. With the door still ajar, Robbie could hear Grace talking earnestly.

"Yes, that's right," she was saying, "He left here last Thursday morning."

There was a pause as the person on the other end of the line talked.

"Oh dear," Grace replied, "I'm sorry to hear that. I'm afraid I don't know what to say."

There was silence again while Grace listened. She then wrote something down on a little notepad.

"Well, if I think of anything, I'll give you a call," she finished, preparing to hang up, "Goodbye."

She stood perfectly still in the hallway for a few seconds before composing herself and returning to the kitchen. What a strange phone call, she thought.

"Everything alright?" asked Robbie, showing concern, "You look a bit peaky there Mrs. Thomas."

"Oh, I'm fine," Grace shrugged, "It's just that one of my guests appears to have gone missing."

She quickly explained that Mr. Brown hadn't turned up for work on Monday, and having enquired with neighbours, his boss had found that he hadn't been seen since leaving the house with his suitcase over a week before. That was the day when he had caught the train for his visit to the Sandybank Guest House.

"So what do you reckon happened to him?" the young fisherman asked, looking concerned, "Do you think he's got a secret lover somewhere that he's run off with?"

"Mr. Brown?" chuckled Grace, "No chance. He's more likely to be train-spotting at the railway station. You've been reading too many Mills and Boone stories!"

Robbie laughed. "I'd better go and help my Dad with the nets," he smiled, standing up and stretching, "Thank you for the tea and cake Mrs. Thomas and I hope your guest turns up alive and well."

Grace opened the back door for the young man and made brief arrangements for him to bring her a 'Catch of the Day' the following week.

After closing the door, she turned her thoughts back to Mr. Brown.

While Grace had been chatting and pondering, Dick had sorted out his horse racing bets and was downing his second pint in the Miner's Pride. Being Good Friday he was surrounded by fellow drinkers, as many of his friends had either been given a day off or finished at lunchtime. The pub chatter was the total opposite of the conversation that had been occurring in Dick's kitchen, and mainly consisted of football scores, horses and the new busty redhead that had recently been employed behind the bar.

"I'd better get back," Dick told his cronies, "I've got an errand to do at the butcher's."

One of the group roared with laughter, "Hah, Dick, you're a rum one with your errands!"

Dick brushed off the comment as foolish and supped the last mouthful of stout,

"I'll see you tomorrow Alf," he chuckled, clapping the bloke on the back, "Let's see if we can win some big money on the Gold Cup this weekend."

Meanwhile, Grace had started preparing the fish for dinner. She had assembled the prawn cocktails for starters, and a couple with egg mayonnaise instead of prawns, as she knew from past experience that the children were fussy eaters. She was now stuffing the mackerel with oatmeal and mustard, just as her mother had taught her. The children would be having a slice of chicken pie each, leftover from Grace and Dick's supper the night before. She found it such a pain catering for children, but these particular two were well-mannered and charming, so she really didn't mind too much.

Just as she was garnishing the fish with a slice of lemon, the door opened and Dick walked in carrying two parcels. Grace sincerely hoped that they contained the lamb for her Sunday roast.

"Here you go dear," Dick proclaimed proudly, "Two legs of lamb."

Grace let out a sigh of relief. Thank goodness he hadn't messed up this time although, looking at the state of him, she couldn't help wondering how much cash he'd spent at the Miner's Pride.

"Thanks", she said, trying hard to look past her husband's dishevelled appearance, "Now why don't you go and have a nice hot bath and make yourself look smart for our guests. I'll bet they'll have lots of luggage and will need your strong arms to help them."

Dick felt like nothing more than relaxing in a hot bath, he could take his half-read newspaper and a cup of tea up with him. He nodded at his wife and raised his eyebrows.

"That sounds smashing," he murmured, giving Grace a quick squeeze around the waist.

"Get off, you daft lump," Grace laughed, "Oh, and while I think of it Dick, there was a phone call about Mr. Brown earlier. He's gone missing apparently."

Dick shook his head. "Well, I don't know anything about it."

"He checked out as arranged?" asked his wife, "And he signed the register?"

Dick rolled his eyes. "Of course he signed the register."

Grace was satisfied with her husband's answers. After all, she trusted him to check their guests out in the correct way. And the bill would have been settled down to the last penny, especially by someone as cultured and well-mannered as Mr. Brown.

She turned back to her food preparation and smiled. Maybe in months to come, friends and relatives of the mysterious Mr. Brown would reveal that he had become embroiled in a love affair and was suspected of eloping with the woman of his dreams, just as Robbie had suggested, she mused.

Easter weekend was just as busy as Grace had expected. She loved playing the perfect hostess and the Sandybank guests were full of compliments from the comfortable rooms to Grace's excellent cooking. She hardly saw the newlyweds, except for mealtimes, but that was only to be expected. The family popped in and out, running down to the beach, coming back to change out of their sandy clothes, trotting back into town for ice-cream and candy floss and then back again for their dinner. Grace loved to spoil the children and had bought them each a chocolate egg for Easter, which caused them to give her a tight hug, making her feel warm and happy inside.

The other guests spent more time than usual in the large communal sitting room in the evenings, due to the unpredictable weather, either reading or playing board games. Grace sometimes joined them, but mostly left them to their own pursuits. The two single gentlemen, both in their mid-sixties, were keen walkers and often retired soon after dinner due to the copious amounts of fresh air ingested into their lungs in the daytime. The other couple had been to the Sandybank on a regular basis for the past five years, a getaway break while their relatives looked after the kids, they said. Grace couldn't imagine going on holiday and leaving the children behind, but then again, she'd never had to deal with temper tantrums or wet beds. She could see that the couple were very romantic towards each other, a kiss here and a squeeze there, something which caused her to reflect upon her own relationship more times than she comfortably cared to.

Dick kept out of the way for most of the time, which his wife didn't mind. But he was always there to help carry luggage, help with the washing-up or just to make Grace a cup of tea when she needed one. He'd made a good job of tidying the front garden the week before and the guests commented on how beautiful it looked, with the daffodils in full bloom and the lawn a vibrant shade of green. Dick liked the guest house being busy, mainly because it always meant that Grace was happy. He realised that it was hard work for her but, as she'd often told him, Grace was in her element when she was entertaining. Dick had to admit that his wife had really excelled over Easter. The meals had been superb and he'd indulged in second helpings on more than one occasion.

It was over those few days, with guests coming and going, that Dick happened to take particular notice of one of the gentlemen guests. He was a very suave and sophisticated man, retired but still with a youthful complexion. Dick had noticed that the man was clean-shaven every day and used a distinctive cologne that reminded him of wood shavings. Henry Patterson had noticed Dick too, but for all the wrong reasons. He had noted the paunch belly hanging over Dick's trousers, the fact that his green cardigan always seemed to be buttoned up incorrectly and the man's scruffy tartan slippers that made a scraping sound on the wooden hall floor as he walked. Henry Patterson had also noticed Dick eyeing him up and down and wondered if he could assist in helping Dick to smarten himself up. A difficult subject to broach, he thought, but Dick had such a friendly face and was probably considered to be extremely handsome a decade ago. And so, over the course of the next few days, Mr. Patterson made it his mission to sort Dick out.

It wasn't until Saturday evening that an ideal opportunity to mention men's fashion occurred.

Grace had been invited to join an after dinner game of Chinese Checkers with the couple, Mr. and Mrs. Lovett, and the other single gent, Mr. Reeves. She had produced a half decent bottle of red wine and the four now sat around the coffee table ready to begin, amidst much laughter and light conversation.

Dick, not being one to miss chances, had seen this as an ideal time to go for a few pints at his favourite watering hole and was slowly sneaking out through the back door. At exactly the same moment, as luck would have it, Henry Patterson was just letting himself out through the front door. The two men came face to face at the top of the garden path.

"Oh, sorry, nearly bumped into you there Mr. Patterson," chortled Dick, making light of the meeting, "Are you off to the local pub?"

"Good evening Mr. Thomas," came the response, "No, actually I'm off to watch a French film at that little cinema on the parade."

Dick was a little taken aback and stifled a laugh, "Oh, right. So you can understand it can you?"

"Well, most of it," Henry Patterson went on, "But they have subtitles at the bottom of the screen too."

"Well I never," Dick exclaimed, genuinely surprised. "They think of all sorts these days don't they?"

The older man grinned at Dick's naivety. "Anyway, where are you off to this fine evening?"

As they fell into step on the walk downhill, Dick explained his escape plan and how he was joining his pals for a few swift pints. Henry liked Dick's honesty but, never having been married himself, he couldn't imagine having to find excuses to sneak out of the house just because you fancied a little tipple. The conversation turned to general talk about the weather and how busy the seaside town had become so early in the year. It was after a few minutes of general chatter that Henry decided to drop a hint.

"I say Dick, have you never thought of wearing a cravat under your shirt collar instead of a tie?" he ventured, "All the chaps in the city are wearing them. A darn sight more comfortable I say."

Dick turned to look at the dark blue paisley cravat that his companion was wearing around his neck.

"Can't say I've really thought about it," he admitted, "It does look smart though, Mr. Patterson."

"Oh, call me Henry, please," came the response, "Oh, look, here we are at the cinema. Well, I'll see you tomorrow no doubt, and think about what I said. With a silk cravat, you'd look really dapper."

Easter flew by at the Sandybank Guest House, in a blinding flurry of Full English breakfasts, roast dinners, bed-making, hoovering and hundreds of cups of tea. Grace was quite sad to see her guests leave at the end of what had been a glorious long weekend, but she was glad to see that her money tin was pleasantly full at the end of it. She felt just a tiny bit guilty that she hadn't spent much time talking to Dick, but she knew he'd been happy amusing himself either in the potting shed or down at the Miners Arms.

Grace spent most of Tuesday and Wednesday changing sheets and cleaning rooms that week and it wasn't until after her hair appointment on Thursday that she decided to call in at the bookshop to treat herself to another Mills and Boone paperback. On her way out of the shop, purchase still in hand, she quite literally bumped into Robbie Powell.

"Whoops, Oh I'm so sorry, I nearly knocked you off your feet there," Robbie gasped, putting his hand under Grace's elbow to steady her.

"It was my fault entirely," Grace apologised, catching her breath, "I had my nose in my new book."

She turned the cover for the fisherman to see, revealing a glamorous couple in a passionate embrace.

"Oh, 'The Love Circle'," he read, sounding slightly disappointed, "That's not one of the good ones."

"Well you've rather put me off it before I've even started."

"Sorry," shrugged Robbie, looking down at his feet, "I can lend you a better one if you'd like."

Grace shook her head, "No, it's fine. I'll read this and then we can see whether I agree with your opinion of it. And I must say, I'm rather surprised at your choice of reading material."

Robbie tugged at the woman's arm to pull her out of the shop doorway as customers were trying to get out. He didn't want to discuss this, here in the street, but felt that he really ought to explain.

"Have you got time for a quick coffee?" he asked, surprising himself as the words tumbled out.

"Well, yes I suppose so," Grace ventured, looking at her watch, "We can go to the café just along here."

Settled into an American diner styled booth, Robbie ordered two frothy coffees and two iced buns.

"Goodness me, I'm trying to watch my figure," Grace scolded, unbuttoning her coat and taking off her scarf. She was very fond of the young man but was conscious of people seeing them sitting so close. They chatted easily for a few minutes but after the coffee and cakes arrived the young man flushed.

"Look, there's something you really ought to know about me," started Robbie, nervously playing with the wrapped sugar cubes in a bowl in front of him.

Grace let out a snort, "I'm quite open-minded you know, and I've already worked out your secret."

She felt alarmed at her own brashness and gently put her hand on the young man's arm before continuing. "It's alright with me, if you, you know, if you like men more than women."

"What?!" exclaimed Robbie Powell, jumping out of his seat and rubbing a calloused hand through his hair.

"Do sit down dear," Grace whispered, trying to console the fisherman before people started to look.

Robbie sighed and slid back into the booth. "Are you mad," he muttered. "Mrs. Thomas I am not a homosexual. I like women very, very much."

Grace sucked in her breath and considered the possibility that Robbie was in denial. She had no idea how to handle this situation and felt completely out of her depth. Luckily, Robbie interrupted her thoughts.

"Mrs. Thomas, Grace, why would you even think such a thing?"

"Well, it's not every day that a young handsome fellow admits to reading romance novels," she explained, "And besides, nobody has ever seen you out with a lady friend."

"So you've been talking to that gossip-monger Maureen O'Sullivan have you?" Robbie spluttered "I don't have time to take girls out, I'm always trying to help my old man earn money."

Grace blushed and took a clean cotton handkerchief out of her coat pocket. Gosh, it was warm in here.

"And another thing," Robbie continued, feeling the tension between them, "For your information I don't read those stupid Mills and Boone books, I write them!"

Grace felt her mouth open.

"You...You write them?" she stuttered, "Are you having me on Robbie Powell?"

"No, I'm not," came the guarded reply, "It's good money and we need it to keep the fishing boats in top condition. My dad's not been well, so I do this to top up our funds."

Grace sat silently staring at the handsome features on the opposite side of the table, waiting.

"You won't tell anyone will you?" he enquired in a soft, low voice, "I'd be made a laughing stock."

Grace shook her head, still taking in the confession. She sipped her coffee and smiled.

"You know what," she ventured, "I think that's an admirable way to earn money. Do you know how many thousands of women get pleasure from reading those stories? And I'm one of them. Don't you worry yourself love, your secrets safe with me, and always will be."

Robbie smiled, hoping that this lovely lady was one of the few that could actually keep her lips sealed.

He gulped down his coffee and stood up to pay the bill.

"I need to get back, to help Dad," he explained, nodding towards the harbour.

"Oh, yes, of course," replied Grace, realising that their conversation was suddenly over. She pulled her scarf on to cover her hair and stood up to fasten her coat, pulling her leather handbag along the seat.

The middle-aged woman and young man walked towards the door, hardly noticing that a few of the other customers were craning their necks and whispering words behind them. Outside in the fresh sea breeze, Robbie reached out and took Grace's hand.

"Thank you Grace," he grinned, feeling like a heavy load had just been lifted off his broad shoulders.

"Don't be silly," Grace retorted, flapping her free hand at him, "You should be very proud of yourself."

"I'll come up tomorrow with some fish, on the house," Robbie answered.

"You don't need to do that, I can pay you for it. Or on second thought, I'll bake you a fruit cake in exchange."

Robbie laughed and looked towards the fishing boats, "You're on, I'll see you tomorrow."

Grace watched him run across the main road, and leap over the promenade wall. He was a fit young man that was for sure, she thought, looking at his solid frame and muscly forearms as he moved. What I'd give to be ten years younger! A pang of guilt suddenly hit her like an arrow. Oh dear, she scolded herself, whatever was I thinking. Grace looked down at the little paperback that she still held in her hand, it would mean twice as much to her now that she knew who was responsible for the steamy love scenes.

Back at the guest house, Dick had been making some drastic changes.

Armed with a fashion catalogue that he'd found at the side of the sofa, Dick had applied Brylcreem to his thinning hair, put on his best blue shirt and had a shave. He's then opened his wife's wardrobe and taken out one of her silk scarves. It didn't matter to him that it had poppies all over it, he just wanted to get an idea of how it would feel to wear a cravat. He wanted to look smart, just like Henry Patterson. It took a few attempts at folding the silk into a roll before he got the desired effect, but he had to admit, it was much less constricting than wearing a tie and the soft fabric felt lovely against his neck.

Grace let herself in through the back door and took stock of the tidy kitchen. There were no dirty plates or cups to wash, so obviously Dick had been too busy to sit eating and drinking all morning. She peered outside, looking firstly towards the patio and then further down towards the shed. There was no sign of him anywhere. She removed her outer clothing and tucked the Mills and Boone novel between some cookbooks on the kitchen shelf. That will be for this evening, she thought, snuggled up by the fire.

Grace heard a faint thump from upstairs and presumed that Dick was busy fixing the leaking tap in one of the guest bathrooms. She'd been on at him for weeks to get it sorted. In light of the fact that he might actually be doing something useful, Grace opened the fridge and took out some fresh ham and tomatoes with which to make them both a sandwich. As she sliced and buttered bread, the woman heard another gentle thud from upstairs. It didn't perturb her and she carried on with what she was doing.

A few minutes later, with the sandwiches ready and a pot of tea brewing, Grace decided to go up and see how Dick was getting on. Besides, he always liked his tea hot and fresh from the pot. Climbing to the top of the wide staircase, Grace turned right towards the guest bathroom. As she did so, the door opened sharply and a rather red-faced Dick stood gaping at her.

It took a few seconds for Grace to fully realise who and what she was looking at. Was that ridiculous looking man, with a poppy-print scarf tied around his neck really her husband? Wonders would never cease.

"Your lunch is ready," she said calmly, turning to go back downstairs, "But get changed first."

Chapter Four

The Meachams

It was a bright and sunny morning in May.

Grace had been up since dawn, making the most of the fine weather by hanging out her washing early, so that come lunchtime, she would already have it ironed, folded and put away. She liked days like these, where she could get on with things. Dick had sauntered into the kitchen an hour after his wife and, not really having any plans for the day, had drunk two cups of tea and was now ready to take a short stroll down to the newsagents to fetch his daily paper. He was wearing a blue cravat under his shirt but Grace hadn't bothered to comment, she was sure that enough folk in town would do that.

"Do you need anything love?" he enquired, not really expecting Grace to respond.

"I quite fancy some lemon sherbets," she quipped, glancing up from the pastry that she was rolling out.

"Oh, right you are then," sniffed Dick, "I'll be back in half an hour."

Grace didn't bother to look up again, but concentrated instead on getting her short crust to the right depth. She did have a smile upon her lips though, as she contemplated the actual likelihood of her husband being able to make it to the shop and back within thirty minutes.

As it happened, less than a minute after Dick had closed the kitchen door, he was back again, looking very alarmed.

"I think you'd better come and see…." was all he could manage to utter.

Grace quickly rinsed her floury hands under the tap and pulled off her pink cotton apron. It didn't matter what the emergency was, she wouldn't allow anyone to see her outdoors in her pinafore.

"Whatever is it?" she gasped, trotting behind her husband as he lumbered towards the front gate.

Dick didn't answer but merely stopped in front of the house and pointed uphill towards the next, a rather grand, double-fronted Georgian red brick affair.

Just as Grace stopped too, and followed his finger, the face of the female occupant of the house appeared over the wall and waved at them wildly before throwing what appeared to be six or seven china dinner plates down on to the road below. The whole lot smashed into smithereens as they landed on the tarmac amidst what appeared to be an already shattered pile of crockery. The householder then slapped her hands together and marched back indoors. Dick and Grace looked at one another in disbelief, and then another head appeared over the top the wall. It was Ronald Meacham.

"I say, morning Grace, morning Dick," the man shouted cheerfully, in his rather nasal upper-class accent, "Don't mind Millie, she's having one of her little temper tantrums."

Grace was too shocked to answer the greeting and merely stared at the broken china, but Dick wasn't quite so easily shaken and raised his hand in a welcoming gesture before speaking.

"I'm guessing you'll be needing a hand to clear that lot up," he called, nodding his head towards the heap of porcelain, "Could be nasty if a car comes along and drives over it."

Ronald Meacham peered down at the clutter below, and nodded gratefully to Dick, who was already making his way up the cliff road towards his neighbour's house.

"Go and fetch a dustpan and brush then, or on second thoughts a broom and shovel," Dick ordered, not in the least happy that his morning newspaper trip had been so rudely interrupted.

The other man ran up the garden path and disappeared inside.

Grace felt like a nosey bystander now, hovering around on the road with nobody at her side, so she slowly turned to go back to the guest house, leaving Dick to help clear up the mess. Perhaps she'd just make a pot of tea and wait for him to return with the full story, much better than looking too curious, she thought.

As she reached the front door, Grace could hear a tinkling sound as her husband carefully scooped up the broken plates and then Dick's very distinctive laughter as their neighbour obviously tried to make light of the situation. My goodness, she mused, turning the large brass knob, I'd die of embarrassment if Dick and I ever had such a bad falling out as that!

An hour later, with jam tarts made and the teapot gone cold, her husband still hadn't returned and Grace presumed that he'd continued his mission to fetch the daily news. Although it was quite unlike Dick not to come and fill her in on the events next door, Grace wasn't unduly concerned and continued her list of chores with more gusto than ever.

In the meantime Dick had been having an unexpected brew next door with Ronald Meacham.

"Here we go old chap," grinned Ronald, carrying two cups into the sitting room, where Dick had been invited to sit and wait while his neighbour fixed refreshments, "I say, we deserve something stiffer than this, what, after all that kerfuffle outside."

"Tea will be just grand," replied Dick, shaking his head, "I never drink before lunch."

Ronald Meacham chortled loudly, showing his bright pink gums, "Ha, quite right too."

While his host had been busy making tea, Dick had spent a good five minutes looking at the antiques and treasures which filled the room that he sat in. There were oil paintings of huge proportions, gilt clocks, Chinese ginger jars painted with birds and fish whose species he couldn't name and large wooden cabinets with multiple drawers and strange engraving. Never having travelled outside of England in his forty plus years, Dick was entranced to see all these foreign knick-knacks brought together in one place.

"You've got a grand home," he told Ronald Meacham, not feeling remotely embarrassed that he was bringing attention to the fact that he'd been having a good look around, "Some handsome clocks."

"Oh, they're all family heirlooms", smiled his host, "Generations of travellers and traders, bringing home their spoils of war."

Dick raised his eyebrows, the contents of this room alone must be worth a small fortune, he thought.

"Erm, is Millie alright?' he asked cautiously, "She seemed in a bit of a temper earlier on."

Ronald Meacham chuckled nervously and nibbled the end of his thumb nail, "Oh, we're always having our little tiffs old chap, nothing new there. Pity about the dinner service though, it was Royal Doulton."

Dick finished his tea in silence and, a few minutes later, made his excuses to leave.

"Jolly nice to see you," enthused Ronald, jumping up to open the door, "I dare say we'll bump into one another again soon, especially if Millie goes on a smashing spree again."

He guffawed and held the door wide for Dick to pass through, patting him gently on the shoulder as he went. "Jolly smart cravat too," Ronald added, "Just the ticket."

Dick eyed up the other man, waiting for him to say something else, but nothing came.

"See you", he said, nodding at Ronald Meacham, "Take care."

The door closed behind him and Dick stood on the step for a few seconds, wondering what went on behind the curtains of the handsome house. As he cast his eyes upwards, he caught a glimpse of Millie Meacham watching him from a bedroom window. She looked rather glamorous standing there with her pearl necklace and perfectly coiffured hair. She certainly didn't look upset. As soon as the woman caught Dick's eye, she dropped the curtain back into place so that he could no longer see her.

It was lunchtime when Dick returned to the guest house and Grace was in the kitchen heating up some tomato soup as he ambled inside.

"Oh, my goodness," she quipped, "Where on earth have you been?"

"Ronald Meacham invited me for a cup of tea, and then I went down to fetch the paper and got talking to Freddie Fletcher", Dick offered, "Word around town is that Ronald's got a gambling habit."

Grace gasped, "Oh, poor Millie, no wonder she was having that temper tantrum."

"Well, it's none of our business," Dick grumbled, "He seems like a decent enough chap to me."

"Mmm, I bet," his wife muttered under her breath, "Anyway what's with that silly cravat today?"

"Good grief woman, there's nothing wrong with wanting to smarten myself up is there?"

"Not at all", Grace fired back, turning to look her husband in the eye, "Unless you've got another woman you're trying to impress."

Dick chortled and shook his head, "Don't be bloody daft woman, how would I find the time?"

Grace thought this over for a few seconds. Oh, the irony of that comment, the damn fool.

Later that afternoon, as the clouds began to darken the sky, Grace happened to look out of the landing window where she'd been busily dusting her precious Wade figures that adorned the ledge. She could see a blue Mini approaching the cliff road from the harbour and as it drew closer she could make out a pretty young woman in the driver's seat. Goodness, she thought, times were changing, when she was twenty years younger it would have been a very rare sight to see a young lady at the wheel of a car. She stopped dusting for a second and wondered what Dick would think if she asked for driving lessons. As Grace stood there daydreaming, with her feather dusted poised in the air, the blue Mini slowed down and then stopped outside her gate. She wasn't expecting any guests today and wondered who it could be visiting at this time in the afternoon. She turned to go downstairs, smoothing her apron as she did so, and hovered for a few seconds, waiting for the woman to ring the doorbell. Nothing happened.

Wondering if the visitor had gone around to the back door, Grace trotted into the kitchen, but nobody was there either. Feeling confused, she then entered the front sitting room and peered out. Strangely the woman was still sitting in her car, applying lipstick in the mirror. Just then, Ronald Meacham appeared.

As Grace watched the thirty-something gent climb into the little car and give the woman a peck on the cheek, so the phone rang and she was obliged to tear herself away from her position behind the curtain. As she lifted the receiver, the picture of Mr. Meacham kissing the young woman still played in Grace's mind. Therefore it took her a second or two to speak to the caller.

"A single room for a week you say?" she repeated as the person on the other end gave their details, "Oh, it was Mr. Brown who recommended us, how lovely."

She listened, pen poised, as the caller continued.

"Oh, yes, it was very strange how Mr. Brown just disappeared, do you think he had a lady friend?"

Grace concentrated on what the speaker was telling her, it seemed nobody knew where he was.

"That's all booked for you Mr. Wellings," she concluded, getting ready to hang up, "We'll see you next week. Goodbye."

Closing the guest register and popping her pen back into the pot beside the phone, Grace stood thinking deeply for a couple of minutes. How odd that nobody had come looking for Mr. Brown but with no immediate family and very few friends, it seemed that people had simply presumed that the old bachelor had gone off on one his trips to far off lands. He'd done it before apparently, although this was the first time without letting anyone know. Grace wished she had an adventurous spirit too.

"Is it alright if I try one of these jam tarts?" Dick called from the kitchen, rousing his wife from her thoughts, "They look blooming delicious."

Grace sighed and padded towards the kitchen, despite it being a day full of secrets and mystery, you could always rely on Dick to bring you back to reality with a bump!

She found him leaning on the kitchen counter, one hand propping himself up while the other greedily shovelled a whole strawberry jam tart into his mouth. She sighed and gave him a despairing look.

"At least use a plate," she tutted, "You've got crumbs all over the floor now."

Dick managed a half smile, partly due to being occupied with chewing the pastry and partly because he wasn't sure whether Grace was going to go into a full scale rant.

Luckily she wasn't in the mood for lecturing and she turned on her heel to go back into the sitting room where she took up her romance novel to escape from the strange reality of daily life.

A couple of days later, as it was Thursday, Grace set off down the hill for her weekly shampoo and set. It was a dull and rainy day, with dark clouds looming overhead and a chilly bite in the wind.

Grace quickened her step as she approached the harbour wall. It was much colder than she had first thought and her thin mackintosh was doing little to stop the breeze from penetrating her flesh. She had purposely worn trousers as she had been on the receiving end of far too many windy mornings lately, and didn't fancy the added encumbrance of trying to stop a skirt from blowing up and showing her knickers.

"Hi there Grace, bit brisk this morning isn't it?" a male voice shouted from a short distance away.

Grace turned towards the beach, putting a hand up to her headscarf to stop the back part from blowing upwards, and was met by the handsome face of Robbie Powell just a few feet away.

"Hello love," she smiled, "You're not taking the boat out in this weather are you?"

"We've been back for hours," Robbie chuckled, "It was calm at five o'clock this morning."

Grace sucked in her breath as a particularly freezing gust of wind blew in her face, and looked at her watch nervously. It was almost eleven.

"I'll have to get going," she shivered, "I've got my appointment in five minutes."

Robbie smiled and gave a little wave, "Bye Grace, see you tomorrow with your delivery."

Grace flushed and headed towards the hair salon. Why is it that every time I set eyes upon Robbie Powell my legs turn to jelly? she chided herself. But still, he was a pretty good catch. She quietly giggled to herself as the joke sank in, a fisherman, good catch, ha, ha very good.

An hour and fifteen minutes later, Grace opened the salon door and peeked outside. With her hair perfectly done and stiff with hairspray, she certainly didn't want to dash up the road in a rainstorm. Luckily, although it was still very cold and the wind had increased in intensity, it wasn't yet raining and she was safe to venture back up the hill to the guest house. However, as she got half way between the turning for the cliff road and her home, the heavens opened and a downpour descended upon poor Grace as she battled against the wind which blew towards her in strong gusts. She was just about to break out into a run, when an umbrella suddenly appeared above her head and a long, slim hand rested on her arm. Grace blinked and looked up to see who had come to save her in her hour of need.

It was Millie Meacham.

Dressed sensibly in denim overalls and a bright yellow fisherman's jacket, she smiled kindly at Grace.

"Such a dismal day isn't it Mrs. Thomas?"

Grace blinked up at the tall woman beside her and nodded, "We're going to have a week of this before we get any sunshine, according to the weather forecast."

"Must play havoc with the sheep," Millie Meacham went on as the two women strode up the hill, huddled together for both warmth and defense from the rain.

"The sheep?" repeated Grace, frowning.

"Well, their wool must go all spongey and doubled in size," explained Millie, really seeming to believe her own logic, "They must feel ever so strange."

Grace giggled and looked up to see her companion grinning widely, "Ooh, you're having me on!" she said.

Laughing aloud and hurrying upwards, the women arrived at the guest house just a few minutes later.

"Coffee?" enquired Grace, "I've got some custard creams too."

Millie looked at her watch quickly and, putting down her umbrella as they reached the back door, said, "Go on then, that sounds like a lovely idea."

Grace stepped inside and waited for the other woman to follow before closing the door behind her.

"Take a seat, I'll pop some milk on the stove," she enthused, "I think a cold day like today calls for Camp coffee and demerara sugar."

Millie Meacham rubbed her long white fingers together and reached up to hang her wet jacket on the coat hook affixed to the back of the kitchen door. Grace busied herself with making coffee but also discreetly eyed up her guest, who was now pulling out one of the chairs to sit on. There was something rather fetching about the denim overalls, flat lace-up shoes and red and white polka-dot blouse. Grace sighed silently, she had all of those type of clothes in her wardrobe but would never have worn them all together. Millie looked so chic.

Millie Meacham was doing a diplomatic survey of her own. She was fascinated with the 'homeliness' of her neighbour's kitchen, with its old-fashioned cabinets and faded tiles, and despite the room being spacious with high ceilings, it was very unlike her own luxurious home where antique vases adorned the window ledge and the curtains were made up in the latest material from Liberty of London. Still, she liked it here.

With the coffee ready and biscuits on a plate, Grace joined Millie at the table. It was a strange feeling, sitting there casually sharing refreshments, as the Meachams had been next door for at least three years but had done little more than wave a greeting at Dick and Grace.

Grace nibbled on a custard cream as Millie complimented her on having such a lovely home. She smiled kindly and thought back to the day that the Meacham's had moved in. It was a winter's day if her recollection was correct. Ah, yes, that's right, black clouds and muddy footpaths, quite similar in intensity to the glum faces and bad tempers that had accompanied the couple as they arrived separately in their fancy cars. That in itself was funny, Grace thought, spending all that money on petrol when you could travel together instead.

"Just what I needed to warm me up," smiled Millie, raising her cup at her host and rousing Grace from her thoughts, "I've never tried liquid coffee before, but it's jolly tasty."

"It's my favourite," nodded Grace, "And thank you for saving my new hairdo!"

Millie Meacham chuckled, "Anything to oblige dear, and that old brolly is more than big enough for two."

The two women chatted amiably until they'd finished their drinks and then Millie glanced out through the window to see if the rain had stopped. It had, and she made her excuses to leave.

Grace looked at the clock on the wall. It was five minutes to one.

"I expect Mr. Meacham will be waiting for his lunch", Grace commented casually.

Millie turned and looked at her quizzically, "Oh, Ron? Huh, he'll be waiting an awfully long time for me to prepare him something to eat. The day that happens, I dare say Hell will freeze over."

Being, what she considered to be, the perfect housewife, Grace was more than a little taken aback by the comment. Did Millie mean to say that she never cooked for her husband?

Seeing that she had obviously surprised her neighbour, Millie continued, "He prefers to eat out dear. And I'm happy for him to do so."

Grace thought back to the day when she'd seen Ronald Meacham climbing into that little blue Mini. Still, it wasn't any of her business and she just pursed her lips waiting for the other woman to continue.

"The house was my father's you see, so we haven't got around to sorting it out properly yet."

"Oh, I see," Grace replied, not really comprehending anything at all, "Well, I guess it takes time."

A few days after her chat with Mrs. Meacham, Grace was out in the garden snipping chives to put into some egg mayonnaise. The guest house was half full and she had offered to make afternoon tea for an older couple after their stroll on the beach. The other husband and wife and a lone gentleman were out rambling somewhere and no doubt would return hungry and weary, needing hot baths and a substantial evening meal. Anyway, as Grace cut a handful of the herb, she heard loud voices.

"Why don't you just leave?" screeched a woman, "I can't stand the sight of you."

This was followed by a deep laugh, distinctly male and very upper-class. Grace looked around.

Just above the hedge bordering her own garden she could see Millie Meacham at an upstairs window. Her face was red and she held an object firmly in her hands as though she was ready to throw it.

"Not that vase!" the male voiced roared, "It's worth a damned fortune!"

Grace could see Millie laughing now. She put down her garden scissors and stepped a little closer. As she did so, Millie caught the movement in the corner of her eye and stepped back from the window. A few seconds later she had fastened the latch and disappeared from view.

Grace, now deep in thought and still clutching the chives in her palm, picked up the scissors and went indoors. Should she go next door and see if everything was alright? As she stood at the sink rinsing both the chives and her hands, the question that buzzed in her head was suddenly answered. A gentle tap came at the back door, followed by the turning of the handle and then the tear-stained face of Millie Meacham poked her head around the frame.

"Oh, my goodness," exclaimed Grace, "Are you alright dear?"

"Yes," sighed the slender young woman quickly sitting down and starting to pick at the seam of the tablecloth, "I'm fine. I just thought

I'd better apologise for making such a scene. That man drives me to distraction sometimes."

Grace lifted her chin knowingly. She couldn't ever remember a time when she'd been angry enough to throw something at Dick, but he certainly made her blood boil sometimes. "Let's have a cuppa," she offered half-heartedly, knowing full well that she only had half an hour before her guests would be returning and expecting tea and sandwiches to be served.

"Thank you," smiled Millie, "But don't let me be a bother if you're busy."

"Nonsense," whispered Grace, "But let me just see to my paying guests first."

An hour later, Millie Meacham was still sitting in the Thomas's kitchen. She had watched Grace prepare a plateful of mixed sandwiches and display them on a china stand, followed by the warming of a teapot and the laying out of cups and saucers on a tray. It amused her how much care the landlady took over what seemed to her to be a menial task, but at the end of the day Grace seemed happy, which was something she doubted could ever be said about herself.

Eventually, with her house guests served, Grace returned her attention to the woman in her kitchen.

"Is there anything I can do to help?" she asked, rather hoping for an answer in the negative form.

Millie flexed her long fingers and inspected her beautifully manicured nails, "Not unless you're willing to hit Ron over the head and bury him under your patio."

Grace started to chuckle but then realised that the woman at her table wasn't joking.

"But surely you don't hate him that much?" she gasped, "I mean, can't you sort things out?"

Millie frowned, a great furrow of lines appearing across her forehead, "No, Grace, it seems impossible. He won't leave the house and neither will I, it seems we're at a stalemate."

Grace, having been brought up to greatly respect the sanctity of marriage, took the younger woman's hand in her own and searched her eyes for some semblance of regret or compassion. They sat in silence for a few moments until the door opened and Dick lumbered in.

"Everything alright love?" he queried, looking back and forth at the two women, "Has someone died?"

Grace pulled her hand back across the table in embarrassment. Immediately she did so, Millie jumped up to leave. By now she was looking much more composed and her natural peachy glow had returned.

'Don't go on my account," continued Dick, "You ladies carry on chatting."

"Oh, it's fine," Millie gushed nervously, "I have to get back, I've got things to do."

With a quick glance back at Grace, she disappeared through the door that Dick was still holding open.

Grace shook her head before Dick could say another thing, "I'll tell you later," she huffed.

That evening, with a substantial meal of steak and kidney pie, boiled potatoes and carrots served up for her guests, Grace stood at the sink washing up the plates while Dick stood to her right, drying them.

"So, what was all that earlier on?" Dick asked cautiously, not wanting to get his head bitten off.

"Oh, it seems the Meachams are not getting on," Grace calmly replied, "I can hardly say I'm surprised."

Dick stood perfectly still with the tea towel poised in his right hand, "Why's that then?"

"I, erm, well I saw something the other day."

Dick turned to face his wife and waited while she gathered her thoughts.

"I saw Ronald get into a car, a Mini I think it was, and I also saw him kiss the driver on the cheek."

Dick sucked in his breath. "You don't think old Ron's a poofter do you!"

Grace tutted, sometimes Dick could be so stupid. "It was a woman driver you silly fool!"

"Oh, that's alright then," he chuckled, picking up a couple of forks from the draining board.

"It most certainly is not alright," retorted Grace indignantly, "Millie was in quite a state today."

Dick frowned as he shoved the forks into the cutlery drawer, "Why's she upset?"

"Well obviously she's found out," Grace sighed, beginning to lose her temper with Dick's slow wits and carefree attitude, "She must have seen him with another woman."

"Well, why would that upset her?" Dick asked, scratching his stomach.

"Oh, for goodness sake! Why don't you go to the pub and drown that brain of yours in beer?!"

"Good idea," grunted Dick, not really needing an excuse to leave the house but feeling ten times better for having one. He really didn't understand why his wife was getting her knickers in a twist.

Struggling into his jacket, Dick bent to give Grace a kiss on the cheek but she turned rapidly away and pretended to get something out of the cupboard. One more word and Dick could see that World War Three would break out, so he grabbed his cap and silently left.

Grace threw a metal colander on top of her baking tins and waited until her growing rage had subsided. If Dick thought that having an affair was alright, what did that say about the state of her own marriage?

It was after eleven when Dick eventually entered the bedroom and flicked on the lamp beside the bed. A book lay open upon the top cover and a pair of glasses were still perched on the end of Grace's nose. She roused slightly when the mattress shifted under Dick's heavy frame as he sat down to take off his socks.

"Are you awake love?" he asked, putting a hand on her arm.

"No, I'm asleep," she murmured, which set Dick off into a fit of laughter.

"Ha, ha, you must be awake if you answered me," he chuckled, "I just wanted to say I'm sorry."

Grace rolled onto her back and opened a heavy lid to reveal one sleepy eye.

"Do you even realise what you've done to upset me?" she muttered.

Dick shook his head, "Not a clue, but I'm hoping you'll tell me."

"You're condoning adultery", she whined, pulling off the spectacles and struggling to sit upright.

"What adultery?!" Dick cried, leaping up from the bed and standing with his hands on his hips.

"Ronald Meacham, with that woman in the Mini, who else?"

Dick looked confused for a couple of seconds and, when reality dawned on him, he started laughing again.

"Ha, you thought that Ron and Millie were married!" he exclaimed presently.

Grace was flabbergasted, "You mean they're living in sin?"

"No, you daft woman," he went on, "They're brother and sister. The house and all its contents were left to them by their father and it's all worth a fortune. Neither one can afford to buy the other out and they both want to keep their old man's house, so they're forced to live together."

Grace didn't quite know what to say and sat in a stunned silence.

"Is it alright if I get some sleep now?" Dick chortled.

"Of course," snapped Grace, smoothing the covers. She was extremely annoyed at Dick for not having mentioned this discovery before her conversation with Millie Meacham.

"Get into bed," she grunted, "And for goodness sake Dick, get rid of that ridiculous cravat."

Chapter Five

Old Mrs. Cole

Mrs. Cole had one of the kindest faces you could ever wish to see. Her eyes positively twinkled as customers entered her little sweet shop and it was almost certain that more purchases were made than most people planned due to the friendliness and laughter exhibited by the tiny shopkeeper. Strategically positioned on the seafront, opposite the very best part of the beach, Mrs. Coles' shop was filled with every type of delicious candy you could ever wish to purchase. There were sticks of rock in multi-coloured stripes, toffee apples wrapped in cellophane and just about every kind of chocolate you had ever set your eyes upon. At the far end of the counter stood a very special glass-fronted display cabinet, full of handmade truffles for those with a more discerning palate and deeper pockets.

Mrs. Cole was very tiny in stature, under five feet tall and as delicate as a china doll. Her hair was pure white with silvery grey tones and as soft as duck down feathers, while her pale porcelain skin bore only the faintest of lines, despite her age of some seventy plus years. It was a mystery to the residents of the seaside town as to why she was called 'Mrs' Cole, when nobody actually remembered there being a 'Mister' Cole. If you'd asked one of the more senior townsfolk, they might have recalled her being married during the First World War some forty odd years ago, but sadly her betrothed had never returned and no other suitor had managed to take his place. The fact that she was also slightly deaf gave her the aura of a cute and lovable grandmother.

Dick was very fond of Mrs. Cole, and he often volunteered to help with odd jobs that needed doing around both the sweet shop and the old lady's home at the rear. He was far happier painting shelves or repairing the fence for the sweet shop owner than he ever was at home, as down here he could work at his own sedentary pace without being nagged at or talked to for hours on end. He never expected to be paid, far from it, but kindly Mrs. Cole would always put aside a little box of her dark chocolate truffles for when Dick had finished his work. In fact, Mrs. Cole never actually asked Dick to do anything for her, it was always he who offered, not wanting anything in return, but he never refused the chocolates either.

Of course, Grace knew the old woman quite well, and she always bumped into her on her Thursday trips to the hair salon, as Mrs. Cole had a regular appointment at half past eleven, the time when Grace herself would be seated under the drier, curlers in and a magazine in her hands. It was a standing joke between herself and Maureen that Mrs. Cole would be asleep within minutes of arriving, and knowing looks often passed between the two at exactly the moment when the old woman's little white head started to nod. Maureen had told Grace about the old lady's peculiar habit of always paying for her hair in loose change, all jumbled up and tipped straight out of her handbag, like she'd been collecting it up for weeks.

Grace didn't often have time to venture into town but, when she did, she would always call in to say "Hello" or to buy a few Imperial Mints to put on the coffee table for her guests. Grace did have quite a sweet tooth herself, but she valued both her figure and her teeth, therefore rarely indulged in the vast array of delights on offer. Besides, she knew that she wouldn't be able to stop at just one chocolate.

The cottage at the back of the sweet shop was just as pleasant and small as its owner. The downstairs consisted of a cosy kitchen with open range and painted cabinets, with a door leading to the comfortable sitting room at the rear. Off this room were a pair of double doors which could be opened in the summer to allow both light and sunshine flow through. The lawn beyond was immaculate, and Mrs. Cole loved nothing more than sitting with her feet up on the sofa in the summer evenings, watching the seagulls swooping down onto the bird table to collect the seed and breadcrumbs that she had scattered for them. Her neighbours worried that the old lady might be lonely, but Mrs. Cole never showed it. Instead, she went about her business, both professional and personal, with an air of enjoyment as if the world were perfect.

Now, the only job that Dick didn't offer to help the shopkeeper with was mowing the lawn. He wasn't quite sure who did that chore, or even if Mrs. Cole herself pushed the mower up and down, but it seemed that at some time over each weekend, the grass had been cut, leaving the garden looking immaculate. Dick had offered to trim the grass on several occasions, but the old lady had always put a tiny hand on his arm and smiled, whispering "Don't worry Mr. Thomas, it's already been taken care of."

One morning, about a week after the argument with Grace following what she now referred to as 'The Meacham Incident', Dick was taking his usual stroll into town to fetch the morning paper when he noticed that the sweet shop door was displaying the 'CLOSED' sign. He stood for a few seconds wondering what to do. It was past nine o'clock and he knew that old Mrs. Cole was meticulous in making sure that she opened at nine on the dot. Dick looked upwards to the window above the shop. The pale pink curtains were still closed. It was pointless knocking the door, he thought, due to the old lady's poor hearing.

Dick decided that he had better go around to the back of the shop, to the door of the cottage, and knock. If the sweet shop owner was ill or, heaven forbid, had taken a fall on the stairs, she would need help he reasoned and therefore it was his duty to go and find out.

Opening the latched gate at the bottom of the alleyway, that separated the sweet shop from the hardware store next to it, Dick stopped to listen. No sound came from inside the cottage, so he proceeded to the back door and knocked as heavily as he could without making the door vibrate.

"Who is it?" chirped Mrs. Cole's voice from inside, as she fumbled with the lock.

"It's only me," replied Dick, "Just come to see if you're alright Mrs. Cole."

The door opened just a crack and the old lady peeped out. She chuckled and touched her hair.

"Oh, Mr. Thomas," she beamed, "I'm so sorry, I had a late night. Just give me a few minutes and I'll have the shop open for you."

Dick noticed that the woman was still in her blue cotton dressing-gown and her feet were bare.

"Don't trouble yourself dear," he smiled, "I just came to see if you needed any help."

Just then there was a scraping sound from inside, like a chair being pulled across the floor, and the old lady suddenly glanced behind her. She quickly looked back at Dick, now slightly flustered.

"Silly cat', she laughed, "You can see that I'm quite well Mr. Thomas, so I'll go and get dressed now."

Dick took the hint to leave and sensed Mrs. Cole watching him as he turned to go back down the alley.

In all his years of living in the guest house, that was the first time that Dick had known the sweet shop owner to be late getting up. Still, he mused, she was getting on in years and the long hours standing behind the counter were probably starting to catch up with her. Dick continued on to the newsagents and by the time he had placed a few bets and strolled back home, the incident with Mrs. Cole was completely forgotten.

Grace had been busy as usual. Mr. Wellings had arrived earlier than expected and having travelled for quite a few hours, he was now seated in the living room waiting for a pot of tea. In his mid-fifties, the visitor was quite unlike the usual single gentlemen that stayed at the Sandybank. Although short in stature, Josiah Wellings was flamboyant in his attire and, on opening the front door to him, Grace was quite taken aback by the burgundy polyester suit and matching Trilby hat. Underneath his suit, Josiah wore a tightly fitted white shirt and a tie patterned with hearts and flowers. Grace had also noticed the gold rings on his fingers and the overly pointed Winkle-picker shoes on his feet.

"Darling, helloooooo", Josiah Wellings had gushed as he entered the hallway, "So lovely to meet you."

Grace had held herself rather stiffly as the little man pecked her on the cheek and dropped his scruffy brown suitcase on the floor, looking around at his surroundings as he did so.

"I'm absolutely parched my love," he'd continued as she showed him up to his room, "I don't suppose there's any chance of a cuppa and a biscuit or two?"

Grace was now preparing the tea for her guest, with a slightly amused smile playing on her lips. She imagined that Mr. Wellings was going to be a fun to have around, although she rather hoped that the other guests didn't take umbrage to his brashness and rather feminine mannerisms.

Dick arrived home just as Grace was carrying the tea tray into the sitting room, and he quickened his step in order to hold the door open as she passed through. It was then that he caught sight of the guest.

"Ow do," he nodded, as Josiah Wellings jumped up from his chair, "Nice to meet you."

"Oh, I say, hello dear," came the response, "Mrs. Thomas didn't tell me she had such a strapping husband."

Grace coughed and set down the tray, rattling the cup and saucer as she did so. She immediately knew that Dick would say something inappropriate and ushered him out into the hallway.

"Now, don't you say a word," she warned her husband as he started to chuckle, 'Mr. Wellings is a paying guest, and I'll not have you making comments about his, erm, unusual ways."

Dick didn't bother to reply but simply sauntered outside to his potting shed to read the paper in peace.

Meanwhile, Grace had returned to the sitting room to see if her guest had any special requests for meals during his stay.

"Oh, lovey, I'll eat whatever you put in front of me," smiled the man in the polyester suit, "Ernest, erm, Mr. Brown, told me what an amazing cook you are."

"Oh, yes, I'd quite forgotten that you knew, sorry I mean know, Mr. Brown," Grace replied, pouring her visitor another cup of tea, "Have you heard anything from him, since he disappeared?"

"Not a peep," Josiah Wellings snorted, waving his hand dismissively, "Not even so much as a postcard."

"Don't you think that's strange?" asked Grace, straightening up.

"Not really dear", her guest tutted, raising his eyebrows, "He goes off on these little trips sometimes."

Grace didn't quite know what to say, and made her excuses to return to the kitchen, promising to have something delicious on the table at six o'clock.

"Oh, I shall so look forward to it", Mr. Wellings sighed elaborately.

Grace retreated and stood in the hallway thinking for a few moments. She hardly dared let the notion cross her mind, but could it be possible that Mr. Brown and Mr. Wellings were more than just friends? No, don't be silly, she told herself, Mr. Brown was nothing like this other guest, he was a scholar and a gentleman, someone to be revered by his work colleagues. Still, she thought, I wonder how they met.

A little later, while Grace was in the kitchen preparing a cottage pie for her guests, the doorbell rang. However, before she could answer it, Josiah Wellings had jumped up from his comfy chair in the sitting room, where he'd been engrossed in a magazine, and raced down the hall to greet the caller.

"Mrs. Thomas sweetie," he called, turning to face Grace as she opened the kitchen door, "There's a rather handsome young man here who appears to be lost."

Grace could see a tall and very good-looking individual, with tanned muscular arms, standing on the step looking bewildered by the other chap's excitement and exaggerated motions.

"Hello dear," Grace smiled, sidling up to Mr. Wellings, who was in absolutely no rush to move aside.

"Good afternoon," replied the young man, smiling widely to show perfect white teeth, "I'm looking for Lavender Cottage."

Grace paused before answering. She didn't have a clue where that was.

"I'm sorry," she told him, "I can't say I've heard of Lavender Cottage."

The man looked down at a piece of paper that he held in his hand and looked puzzled.

"Oh," he shrugged, "That's what it says, Mrs. Cole, Lavender Cottage."

Grace suddenly brightened as if a light had been switched on inside her head, "Oh, Mrs. Cole! I'm so sorry dear, I completely forgot the name of her house. We just know it as the sweet shop."

Josiah Wellings flapped his hands excitedly, "Oh, well done, Mrs. Thomas, well done."

He moved himself behind Grace so that she could point towards the harbour and give the young man directions to the old woman's shop.

"Are you a relative?" Grace asked, feeling a little bit cheeky but interested at the same time,

"No, I'm answering her advertisement for a gardener."

Grace sucked in her breath, she wasn't aware that Mrs. Cole was hiring help. Why hadn't she just asked Dick to mow the lawn if she felt she couldn't manage?

Josiah Wellings, eager to get back to his magazine and fifth cup of tea, put his hand on the door.

"Lovely to meet you," he chirped, turning the handle, "Bye bye for now, sweetie."

Grace and her guest watched the tall figure stride back down the hill towards the town. He was very athletic and looked more than capable of taking care of Mrs. Cole's flower beds.

Grace mentioned the caller to Dick that evening.

"Humph, she only had to ask me," Dick grunted, "Must have more money than sense."

"Well, perhaps she didn't want to put on you," Grace replied, "Besides, you've got more than enough jobs to do around here, without running around after other people."

Dick rolled his eyes and took another mouthful of cottage pie.

"I mean, the patio still isn't finished yet," his wife continued, hoping that at some point Dick would surprise her and get the damned thing completed, "And the weather forecast is good for the next few weeks."

Dick pretended not to hear and cleared the food on his plate.

At that point Grace gave up trying to get a response and got up to clear the table.

"I'll do a bit tomorrow," Dick finally muttered, "Depending on the weather."

Grace started to run water in the sink and smiled. He always gave in, you just had to handle him right.

An hour later, with Dick gone to the pub and her guests settled in their various pursuits, Grace sat down in her own private sitting room with another new romance novel. She had just reached the third page when a face appeared around the door.

"Hello love, I did knock but you obviously didn't hear me," gushed Mr. Wellings, "I was wondering if your hubby fancied a game of cards."

Grace smiled weakly and closed her book, "He's gone out, I'm afraid, but I wouldn't mind playing."

"Ooh, gone out you say?" quizzed the little man, bouncing on the spot as he spoke, "Anywhere interesting?"

"Just the local pub dear, he goes down there for a pint most evenings."

Josiah Wellings puffed out his bird-like chest, "I quite fancy a pint myself actually, enjoy your book."

With a back-handed wave the little man disappeared and could be heard letting himself out through the front door. Very strange, thought Grace, how very strange indeed.

A couple of hours later Grace pricked up her ears as she heard the gate swing on its hinges. Both Dick and their unusual guest were back, chatting loudly as they entered the hallway and obviously a bit worse for wear. She set down her glasses and waited. One set of footsteps could be heard going upstairs.

"Ah, here you are my precious!"

Grace cringed as Dick lumbered towards her, fully intending to plant beer-soaked kisses on both her cheeks. Moving quickly to avoid her husband's embrace, she frowned and went out to the kitchen.

"Hic, hic," Dick gulped, following his wife down the hallway, "I think I need a glass of hic, hic, water."

"Do you really think that's good for business?" Grace rounded on him as Dick made to sit down, "I mean for goodness sake, you're three sheets to the wind."

Dick smiled widely at his wife and patted his knee with his large hands, "Come and sit here and give me a cuddle", he grinned, "You know hic, you want to."

"Grrr, get a glass of water to get rid of those hiccups. And take a blanket out to the potting shed!"

As Grace stormed upstairs to bed, Josiah Wellings silently let himself out of the little guest bedroom with a bottle of cherry brandy in his hand. As far as he was concerned, Dick hadn't finished drinking yet.

The next morning, Grace was up with the lark, preparing breakfasts and laying out information leaflets for her guests. There were so many things to see and do around her beautiful coastal town that she wanted everyone to enjoy their stay to the limit. The weather was starting to get warmer and this particular morning, the sunshine blazed down on the front garden, show-casing the pretty border flowers and adding a glow to the lightly scented magnolia now in bud around the front door.

Most of the guests were up bright and early, something which pleased Grace no end as it gave her chance to make the beds and start her chores straight after breakfast service. There was a light hum of voices coming from the dining room as people conversed pleasantly over boiled eggs and cornflakes. The only guest who hadn't yet arisen was Josiah Wellings. Everyone presumed that he was in bed with a hangover.

By nine o'clock, tables were cleared, crockery washed and put away, and guests scattered to pursue their various activities. One lone place-setting remained intact in the dining room, waiting for the late riser in the house to come downstairs and seek sustenance. Grace had no intention of chastising Dick about getting drunk the night before, after all she much preferred to have him out from under her feet in the evenings, but she would be having serious words with him about fraternising with the guests. As she pondered how best to tackle her husband, Grace caught a glimpse of movement at the bottom of the garden and a large figure emerged from the shed. Dick straightened up and stretched, but on noticing Grace, scuttled back inside his safe haven and closed the door.

Grace pretended not to care, he'd have to come out, eventually...

It wasn't long before Grace had the house ship-shape and her guests sorted out with day trips and walks. It was at this point that Dick finally emerged, looking sheepish and embarrassed.

"Look love, it was a few beers and a little night-cap..." he explained gently, "No harm done."

Grace didn't speak but eyed him dubiously, this wasn't the first time that Dick had acted foolishly.

"Look, why not pop up to your Mum's for the day?" he continued, putting an arm around his wife's shoulder, "You wouldn't need to be back until about four. I can set out some pots of tea and biscuits if anyone needs a snack later."

Grace stood stiffly with her arms folded and thought through his words. Maybe it would do her husband good to take responsibility for once. Yes, why not, she would take a day off! After all, she deserved it.

"Right you are then", she sniffed, giving Dick a sidelong glance, "Don't forget to hang out the washing when it's done, and listen out for the phone. We can't afford to miss any bookings...."

Dick smiled, a childish goofy grin that made Grace's heart melt. She loved her husband, but today he would get to learn a lesson, he would see what she had to cope with every day. And later, Grace would pick up the pieces and correct all the things he'd done wrong.

Pulling her coat on quickly, hardly daring to believe that she was taking a day off, Grace straightened the leather ledger before disappearing out through the front door. First she would head to town to pick up a few things for her parents, and then back up the hill for the half hour walk to their bungalow.

As soon as the front door closed, Dick ambled back to the kitchen to make a pot of tea. He stood at the sink filling the kettle and signalled to Josiah Wellings, who was peering around the potting shed door.

In town, Grace had decided upon flowers for her mother and a box of nut truffles for her father. She now stood patiently, with one hand on the sweet shop counter, as old Mrs. Cole carefully wrapped the chocolates in pale pink tissue paper and sealed the package with a little gold sticker.

"Did that nice young man find you the other day?" Grace asked casually, trying to make conversation.

"Who?" quizzed the old lady, looking up from her task, "What young man?"

"Said he was looking for you, something about mowing your lawn I think."

"Oh, Timothy," the elder woman tutted, "He wasn't very good, I've got another chap now."

"You know," started Grace, wondering how to tactfully offer her husband's services for free, "Dick could always find time to do it for you."

Mrs. Cole eyed Grace carefully, "Oh, no need. It doesn't take these young fellows long at all."

"But still..." Grace pushed, not noticing that her offer was being firmly rejected, "Dick wouldn't charge you anything and he's got plenty of free time."

"Oh, how very kind, but there's really no need." The reply was abrupt and final.

Grace popped the gift into her open bag and eyed the shopkeeper warily. There was no hint of malice or ungratefulness in her face, Mrs. Cole was still smiling and her eyes were still twinkling.

"Good day dear," the little pensioner said, moving slowly to display a new batch of toffee apples tied with ribbons in a basket, "I hope your father enjoys the truffles, they're my favourites."

Grace bid the woman good day and stepped back out into the sunshine on the busy street. It was turning into a beautiful morning and townspeople bustled to and from their businesses, homes and holiday cottages. She reflected for a moment on how lucky she was to live here, by the sea, and how lucky too, to have never had to move away for the whole of her forty something years. Grace looked back at the sweet shop behind her, with its sparkling windows and pretty displays. Mrs. Cole had been here her whole life too, a great deal longer, and Grace's parents would remember her. She must remember to ask them.

Still, it was a strange thing, the old woman not wanting to accept help from Dick. Perhaps it was a matter of pride, Grace wondered. Although, no, it couldn't be that, as she had quite readily agreed for him to repair the leaking tap last winter, and Dick had told her that he'd been there painting the picket fence around the cottage garden only weeks before. Grace was in a quandary. Had Dick really been helping?

Despite having misgivings about her husband's recent behaviour and also inwardly panicking about what kind of pickle she might return to after her day out, Grace thoroughly enjoyed her visit. Both parents were in good spirits, having recently returned from a couple of days in the city, where they had indulged in lots of shopping and theatre trips. Her mother looked a picture of health as she regaled her daughter with the gossip about who was marrying whom. Grace sat patiently listening, until finally it was time for her mother's attention to turn to fashion.

"You know, those patent boots are all the rage now, Grace darling," she enthused, "You really ought to get some, they'd make your legs look much longer and slimmer."

"Mother, I'm forty-two years old," sighed Grace, all too aware that she was, this very moment, being very harshly judged on her practical cotton dress and Mary Jane shoes, "I'm too old to be following the latest trends, they're for young people."

"Balderdash," her father chipped in, "Look at your mother, she looks like a twenty year old!"

Grace smiled. Mother had always looked a lot younger than her true age, tall, slim and dark, with an enviable wardrobe. Sadly, Grace took after her father, who was both shorter and paler.

"Anyway, we bought you and Dick gifts. What do you think?"

Grace's mother had pulled a red silk scarf out of a paper bag and was holding it up.

"Oh Mother, it's gorgeous," Grace grinned, rushing over to kiss both parents, "I love it."

Her father laughed, "That one's for Dick. It's a cravat. All the city chaps are wearing them."

Grace tried not to let her disappointment show and gave a little shrug, not another blessed cravat!

"And these are for you darling," her mother continued, reaching out to pass Grace a little blue box.

Inside were a pair of hooped earrings, made from green beads and crystals. Not Grace's style at all.

She faked a smile, "Oh, thank you both, you shouldn't have."

"Now, let me drive you home", muttered her father, "Before that husband of yours sets fire to the place, or worse still does nothing all day and leaves you with a house full of hungry guests."

Grace nodded, it was half past three. There had been plenty of time for Dick to mess up and she would only have an hour or so to sort things out before having to start cooking dinner.

Back at the Sandybank Guest House, all was quiet.

The washing was dry, folded and had been put in the laundry basket. Guests who had returned mid-afternoon had been greeted with a fresh pot of tea and assorted biscuits in the sitting room and two more bookings had been carefully registered for the following week.

Grace slipped silently in through the back door and listened with baited breath. She could hear cups chinking upon saucers and the creak of the hall door on its hinges as someone entered.

"Oh, hello love," Dick beamed. He was carrying an empty plastic tray in one hand and a tea towel in the other. Grace smiled and set her bag down on the worktop.

"Everything alright?" she asked dubiously, "Any problems?"

"Nope! Don't think so…" Dick pondered, trying to remember if there was anything he needed to report.

"Oh, well that's good then," Grace smiled faintly, reaching up to the hook on the back of the door to retrieve her cotton apron, "I'll make a start on the vegetables."

Dick slowly let out the breath that he'd desperately been holding on to for the past ten seconds,

"There's tea in the pot," he offered.

Grace smiled broadly, "Great, I'd love one."

Later that evening, as they sat in their own private sitting room, in front of the fire with the radio broadcasting a play, Grace turned to her husband and raised an eyebrow.

"So, where's your new friend tonight then?"

Dick blushed, he knew that she meant Josiah Wellings.

"He's erm, gone down the Miner's Arms again," he muttered, "Anyway, he's not really my friend as such, he chats to everyone down there. And let's not forget he'll be gone in a few days, love. I just find him an easy chap to get on with that's all."

Grace nodded, her usual sarcasm ready to surface at any given moment, "Oh, I see."

Just then there was a loud rap on the door to their private quarters and Mr. Wellings appeared.

"Oh, my giddy aunt," he gushed, wiping his brow with a huge white handkerchief, "You get to hear of all sorts in these little towns don't you dear?"

Grace put down her knitting and turned to face their guest. Dick was already on his feet.

"What's happened?"

"Oh, well not happened exactly," Josiah chirped, "Been going on for ages by all accounts."

Grace feigned indifference but kept her ears alerted for the gossip that she knew would be forthcoming.

"I was just coming back from the pub when I erm, well look, there's no easy way to say this, I needed a tinkle."

"A tinkle...." Dick repeated, blinking at the little man in disbelief.

"Yes, well, sometimes a fellow just has to go," Josiah continued, "Anyway, the only place I could see TO go was down that alleyway by the sweet shop. So, wanting to be discreet, I nipped into the old lady's garden to erm, well, you know empty my bladder."

Grace gasped involuntarily, "Oh goodness! Poor Mrs. Cole. She saw you, didn't she?!"

"Saw me? No she jolly well did not dearie," Mr. Wellings puffed out his little pigeon-chest indignantly, "But I saw her, the dirty mare!"

Dick looked at Grace and Grace continued to stare at their guest.

"She was at it in the kitchen with that young hunk of beef that mows her lawn!" the short man squealed, "There, I've said it now! They were doing allsorts!"

"Don't be silly, she's seventy...."

"Grace, I am telling you sweetie," Josiah breathed heavily, putting a hand on Grace's chair to steady himself, "She's even got a tip pot full of coppers on her window sill!"

Grace formed a huge 'O' with her lips.

Lucky, lucky Mrs. Cole!

Chapter Six

Oscar Renfrew

For a couple of days, Dick and Grace had been getting along better than they had in a long time. Whether out of guilt for his recent escapades or a sudden realisation that he couldn't live without his wife, Dick had been kind and considerate, impacting both Grace's mood and their little business. The atmosphere of recent months had lifted and not one cross word had passed between them.

Of course Dick was still feeling twinges of regret for his drinking binge with their colourful house guest, but after explaining to Grace that it was simply male camaraderie, she had forgiven him. In fact, on the very day that Josiah Wellings had departed from the Sandybank, it had been Dick that had checked the little man out and taken his money. Dick had insisted that he start taking a more active role in the business and, on the morning in question, he had sent Grace into town to treat herself to a new outfit. When she had returned some hours later, with a wide-collared button up shift dress in pale mustard, there were ham sandwiches under a plastic dome on the side in the kitchen and Dick was hard at work in the garden. Beads of sweat trickled down his forehead as he worked.

"Tea love?" Grace called from the kitchen window, as she watched Dick push the shovel into the ground.

The large man straightened his back and looked up to see his wife filling the kettle at the sink.

"Grand", he smiled, "I'll be in in two ticks."

Grace flipped the switch on the radio and swayed her hips as Herman's Hermits proceeded to sing to Mrs. Brown, telling her what a lovely daughter she had.

"I might even have that patio done in a few weeks," Dick grunted, as he opened the back door and padded into the kitchen in his thick woollen socks, "We could sit outside in the evenings then."

Grace smiled. She didn't plan to get her hopes up as Dick had been working on his 'patio project' for a very long time, longer than she cared to calculate, but it was lovely to see him so enthusiastic.

"Don't overdo it," she told him, setting the sandwiches out on the table, "And thanks for making these."

"Let's have a look what you bought then?" Dick muttered, helping himself to some lunch.

"All in good time," Grace chuckled, bringing the teapot over to where her husband now sat, "Anyway, did Mr. Wellings depart on time? No sudden emotional displays of affection?"

Dick shook his head. "Ah, behave woman. He was gone by half nine, just after you. The money for his board is in the pot, minus a pound which I'll put back later, but I haven't been up to get his sheets off the bed yet. Got preoccupied out there." He nodded towards the garden.

Grace stood looking at her husband in awe. That must have been the first time in ten years that he had actually even thought about changing the sheets on a guest bed. Well, she sniffed, wonders will never cease. Secretly she was puzzled as to where the real Dick had gone and if he was coming back!

"I might just have a walk into town this afternoon," Dick started, realising that he hadn't yet been down to put his bets on the horses for that afternoon's races.

Grace let out a soft sigh and smiled, so the old Dick was still in there after all.

She didn't reply, but nodded in acknowledgment and nibbled slowly at her sandwich.

Walking briskly down the cliff road, Dick felt the warmth of the sun on the back of his neck and opened the top button on his shirt collar. It was funny how he seemed to feel the heat more than usual these days, maybe it was those few extra pounds he was carrying. Still, he mused, it was all credit to his wife's cooking, she made him some wonderful meals, not to mention all the sponges and biscuits. Dick had felt his weight gain quite noticeably out in the garden that day, it had been more of a struggle than usual to get motivated and every shovelful of soil he lifted had seemed to set him back in strength. Nevertheless, he had promised himself that, once the patio area was complete, there would be no more projects for a while, only the usual chores around house and garden. Well, that was unless Grace had other plans for his time, which knowing her could be under consideration at that very moment.

Today was a first for Dick, in that he hadn't been down to fetch his newspaper that morning, what with sorting out Josiah Wellings and other things, therefore he hadn't been able to study the form of the horses which would be racing that afternoon. So now, it was with a quick step that Dick strode towards the bookmaker's in the centre of town, knowing full well that he only had half an hour to make his choice before the first race. As he opened the door, the bell tinkled and Oscar Renfrew's cheery face looked up from his position behind the counter, casting a glance at the clock on the wall as he did so.

"What time do you call this?" he chuckled, "Grace been slave-driving you again?"

Dick sauntered towards the bookmaker and picked up a betting slip off the side.

"Not bloody likely, I'm the boss in that house."

Oscar Renfrew chuckled, "Aye, of course you are Dick. Now which nag are you taking in the two fifteen?"

Dick sucked the end of his stubby pencil, he couldn't decide. The horse that he would have picked was now joint favourite, so that meant less money back if it won, he knew he should have come down here earlier. He ran his fat sausage-like forefinger down the piece of paper in front of him, scanning the names, jockeys and trainers. Suddenly he stopped.

"Amazing Grace, ten to one", he read aloud, "That's the one, it's an omen. I'll put a pound to win."

Oscar Renfrew scrunched his face up in disagreement, "Are you sure Dick? A pound's a lot of money, and that horse hasn't won a race for two years."

Dick thought for a moment. A pound was a lot of money, in fact it was more than they charged for a one night stay at the Sandybank, but still, he was feeling lucky and with a slight flourish, he slapped a crispy new note on the counter-top.

"Gone into counterfeiting too have you?" asked the bookmaker, raising an eyebrow, "That's a fake."

Dick looked down at the green paper pound note in disbelief.

"Look, here," urged Oscar Renfrew, pointing at the picture of Her Majesty's head, "The colour's all smudged around the edge of Liz's face."

"But....," started Dick, still not quite believing what he was being shown, "I had that off one of our guests this morning."

The other man stood up and scratched his chin. "Looks like you've been had there old chap. You'd best get on to the police."

Dick was still staring at the pound note, seeing that the forgery was a very obvious one. There were more of these at home, he cursed, taken from Mr. Wellings in payment for his room. And, what's more, it would only be a matter of time before Grace discovered the remainder of the fake money in her housekeeping tin. The repercussion of that was something that he dared not even contemplate right now.

"I tell you what," offered the betting shop owner, "I'll lend you a pound for the bet, we'll listen to the race, and then we can call round at the police station before going for a pint. How does that sound?"

Dick nodded. Grace was going to have his guts for garters. Just when things had been going so well.

"Alright, ta very much Oscar," he agreed, trying to mask the growing tension behind his eyes, "It's alright I know exactly who it was that tried to diddle us. Seems a bit pointless going to the police though."

"That's up to you," his friend smiled, "But you never know, the bobbies might be able to catch him before he cheats some other poor bugger."

As it happened, thirty-five minutes later Dick was jumping for joy, all thoughts of the counterfeit notes put behind him, as 'Amazing Grace' romped across the winning line.

"I knew it!" he cheered, causing several old men to wander over and clap him on the back, "Knew my Grace was a lucky charm. Hand over my winnings Oscar."

The bookmaker grinned, he was genuinely happy for his friend, "There you go," he quipped, counting out the money into Dick's chubby palm, "Minus the pound stake, of course."

"Of course!" laughed Dick, "And thanks again mate, I appreciate that."

"Guess the drinks are on you then," Oscar grinned cheekily.

Dick didn't answer, but headed for the door, closely followed by the betting shop owner who, leaving his business in the capable hands of his assistant, was licking his lips in anticipation of the first pint.

A few hours later, Dick set off back up the hill towards home, his intention of going to the police station now nothing but a distant memory. He hadn't wanted to push his luck with Grace by drinking too much in an afternoon and, besides, he wanted to replace the counterfeit notes in her housekeeping tin with real ones from his winnings before she noticed. He could just imagine the names that she would call him, should she ever find out. Dick still couldn't believe that he hadn't noticed the forgery himself, but he had to admit, he'd wanted to get rid of the annoying little guest as soon as possible. Josiah Wellings had been a good laugh in the pub, and also when they'd drunk brandy and played cards in the shed, but he'd been a little too forward in his effeminate ways for Dick's liking. Too many of those guests and they'd be getting themselves a reputation! He'd found it a bit curious how Oscar had talked him out of reporting the incident, but at the end of the day, Dick wasn't keen on making statements or being interviewed either and agreed to let the matter rest.

Grace was just about to serve up the guests meals when her husband entered the kitchen, and the smell of bubbling fish pie permeated the air. Dick's stomach gave an involuntary rumble, causing him to cast a sheepish look across the room. Grace was far too engrossed in spooning out peas to notice.

"Wash your hands and sit down love," she ordered without looking up from her task at hand, "You might as well eat yours now while it's hot."

Dick went to the sink and rolled up his sleeves, watching Grace disappear into the dining room with plates. As soon as the kitchen door swung back into place, he reached up to the top shelf and took down the metal biscuit tin in which they always kept their guests payments before taking it to the bank every Monday. Quickly removing the bright green pound notes that he had deposited there that very morning, Dick replaced them with used ones from his pocket and slid the tin back into place. He breathed deeply.

"Everything alright love?" Grace chirped, gliding back into the room to collect more meals.

"Oh, aye, yes, yes, couldn't be better," Dick smirked as he pulled out a chair to sit on, "Just grand."

The following day, straight after breakfast, Dick stood reading the shopping list that Grace had made for him. He frowned as he looked at the vegetables written there.

"Courgettes!" he exclaimed, "Who eats them things?"

Grace tutted loudly. "I'm making a side dish with them", she explained, "It's all the rage in France, you mix them with tomatoes and onions and bake them in the oven."

"What's wrong with proper English food?"

"Sometimes our guests expect continental meals Dick and I need to stretch my culinary expertise."

Her husband refused to comment further, instead sticking out the tip of his tongue as he continued reading the items on the list. Satisfied that he knew what he needed to buy from the market, Dick picked up a string bag from the cupboard under the sink and slipped his feet into his boots.

"Don't forget to call in on Mrs. Cole," teased Grace, knowing full well that Dick was far too embarrassed to even enter the sweet shop in light of recent revelations, "Tell her I said hello."

Her husband grunted and slowly pushed his thick arms into his tweed jacket, "I'll be back in an hour."

Grace waited for the broad shoulders of her other half to disappear through the back door before turning her attention to the hoovering. Goodness, how her guests always managed to get crumbs all over the dining room carpet she would never know. Still, they were a friendly bunch this week, all couples and all very easy to please. Everyone had seemed to enjoy their meals and nobody had asked for anything out of the ordinary. A nice easy week, Grace mused, as she pushed the vacuum across the green patterned carpet, moving chairs and tables as she did so. She also wondered if Dick had any further plans to work on the paved area outside this week. How wonderful it would be, she thought, if we could host cocktails on the lawn, with posh martini glasses and olives on sticks. She suddenly realised that she had never actually made a cocktail before, well, except the odd 'Snowball' of Advocaat and lemonade at Christmas. She could ask Miss. Meacham for advice. After all, Millie certainly seemed like she would know how to mix one.

With the vegetables secured in his string bag, newspaper purchased and a few fleeting conversations with the townsfolk, Dick was ready to set off back up the hill when a heavy hand clapped him on the shoulder.

"Alright there?"

Dick turned to see Oscar Renfrew grinning at him from ear to ear.

"Hello, what brings you outside in daylight hours?" he laughed, surprised that his friend wasn't working.

"Just popped out to get a birthday gift for Betty", the bookmaker explained, nodding towards the jeweller's shop across the street, "Thought I'd treat her to something special."

Dick momentarily thought back to the last time he'd seen Oscar's wife, it was a couple of months ago now, when she'd joined them for a Saturday night drink at the Miner's Arms. He'd remembered wishing that Grace would come out and socialise with them. That particular scenario was unlikely to happen however, as firstly she didn't like leaving her guests unattended, and secondly she felt that the local public house was a far from suitable venue for a woman of her high morals. Betty Renfrew, on the other hand, had no such qualms and happily laughed and joked with anyone over a glass of gin.

"What are thinking of getting?" Dick asked, genuinely interested in how other people spent their money.

"No idea yet," admitted Oscar as he fell into step beside his friend, "Perhaps you could come and help me choose something, I mean, that's if you've got time,"

Dick was honoured to be asked his opinion on such an important matter as choosing a spouse's present and he willingly agreed. The two men crossed over the main road, having to quicken their step to avoid an oncoming bus full of tourists. They now stood outside the jewellers, taking in the window display.

"Plenty of choice anyway," Dick observed as he scanned the padded trays, "Some fancy pieces too."

"Oh, I'm not so sure," the other man answered, clicking his tongue as his eyes moved along the frontage, "I was hoping for something a bit more, you know, unique."

"They might have some special bits inside," Dick suggested, moving forward, "Shall we have a look?"

Oscar nodded and followed his chubby friend through the door. The shop was bright and airy, and the men were greeted by the familiar tall figure of Ernest Shaw, whom they'd known since their schooldays.

"Morning," the slender jeweller greeted them, "What are we after today then?"

Dick looked at his companion, who was turning this way and that looking for something to catch his eye.

"I need a birthday gift for Betty...."Oscar explained, "You know what she's like Ern, it has to be something really sparkly and good quality."

The jeweller had obviously had the pleasure of serving Betty Renfrew's tastes in the past, and he put one finger up to his nose, tapping it knowingly.

"I'll get you the 'other' tray out of the safe," he grinned, "Won't be a moment."

Dick quickly turned to Oscar as the two men watched Ernest Shaw disappear from view.

"That sounds expensive!" he whispered, nudging his friend with his elbow.

Oscar seemed unperturbed and simply shrugged, "Nothing's too good for my Betty."

Dick felt slightly embarrassed that he'd made a comment about the price. He was also worried that the bookmaker might think him a cheapskate when it came to his own wife's little luxuries.

"Oh aye," he countered quickly, "That's what I tell my Grace all the time, anything she wants..."

His voice trailed off as Ernest Shaw returned with a large black velvet-covered box and positioned it carefully on the glass display unit. He pressed a little button and the lid flipped open.

"Here we are," the jeweller said proudly turning the box around so that his customers could see the contents, "The finest diamonds, all the way from Amsterdam."

Dick stood open-mouthed, his jaw hanging loosely, creating folds of skin underneath his chin.

Inside the box, neatly lined up on a cushioned pad, were three rows of diamond earrings, all of various sizes and cut, and all very obviously way out of the price range of most of the seaside townsfolk.

Oscar however, seemed delighted with the gems and stood gazing at the glittering jewels for quite a few seconds before he was able to speak.

"How much are those ones?" he finally asked, pointing to a medium-sized pair of crystal cut drop earrings.

Ernest Shaw smiled, "For you, a special price of one hundred pounds Oscar."

"I'll take them," grinned the bookmaker, "Gift-wrapped of course please."

Dick stood fixed to the spot. His brain was desperately trying to calculate how many weeks with a full guest house it would take him & Grace to earn that kind of money. And yet, here was his dear friend Oscar Renfrew spending his hard earned cash like there was no tomorrow. Even more transfixing was the unbelievable moment when Oscar peeled off the notes from a huge bundle in his inside jacket pocket.

Back on the street outside, with Dick still in a state of shock and Oscar oblivious to the confusion in which his friend now found himself, the two men shook hands and parted company.

"See you this evening for a pint?" asked the betting shop owner, "Miner's Arms about seven?"

Dick nodded and eyed his friend up and down, "Alright, seven it is then."

After dinner that evening, as Dick came downstairs in a clean shirt ready to go to the pub, Grace stood in the hallway with the telephone receiver to her ear. She was listening intently and writing in the register.

"Double room, seven nights, arriving next Friday," she concluded, "All booked Mrs. Robinson."

Dick smiled. More guests would mean more money in the bank. Maybe they could afford a few extra treats this month and with Grace's birthday the following month perhaps a special gift too.

"What are you so happy about?" Grace chirped, stirring her husband from his daydreaming.

"Just thinking it's good to have a full house," he smirked, "More money in the pot."

"Well, it's going in the bank for our retirement fund," Grace lectured, giving him a stern look, "So don't you think about frittering it away on trivial things."

Dick sighed, he knew she was right, but hated feeling so financially restricted.

Half an hour later, Dick was coming to the bottom of his first pint. He licked the last bit of foamy froth from his lips and gave a sigh of deep satisfaction. Somehow, the first pint always tasted the best.

"Same again?" asked Oscar, nodding at his friend's empty glass, "My round."

"Well, it'd be rude to say no wouldn't it?" Dick joked as he watched the bookmaker count out coins to pay for their drinks, "I'll get the next round."

Mulling over the events of the day, the weather, the horse racing results and anything else that sprang to mind, the two friends spent an amiable evening drinking and chatting. As closing time came, with the pub landlord ringing the bell loudly and declaring "Time Gentlemen, Please!" Dick and Oscar finished up their beer and made their way outside.

"Fancy a nightcap?" Oscar offered cheerfully, "I've got a good single malt in the flat."

Dick grinned, despite the last 'nightcap' he'd had with their strange little guest, he knew that he was in safe hands with his friend. Besides, Betty Renfrew would put a stop to their shenanigans before they got too rowdy, he was positive of that.

As Oscar turned the key in the door, the smell of beef stew wafted outwards and permeated Dick's nostrils, causing him to salivate. Betty must have left dinner on the stove for her husband, he thought. Settling into a big comfy armchair in the lounge, Dick pulled off his shoes and leaned back while his host fetched glasses for the whisky. The room was modestly furnished but everything looked new and in pristine condition. Even the cushions looked like they'd never been crumpled.

"Here you go," chuckled Oscar, handing Dick a drink, his voice shaky with alcohol, "There's some stew I can warm up if you fancy?"

Dick was never one to refuse a good plate of food and soon the two men were talking loudly and enjoying the slow-cooked meat that Betty had prepared earlier.

"We should get our bicycles out at the weekend," Oscar suggested, "Get ourselves fit and healthy."

Dick couldn't remember the last time he'd done any physical exercise and screwed his nose up.

"What do we want to do that for?" he complained, "There are no other pubs for miles."

Oscar could see that the idea had fallen flat but he pushed his friend a little more, "Come on, it'd be a laugh, we could take our fishing rods and go round the coast road."

Dick started laughing and put down his drink on the coffee table, "Can you imagine us on bikes!"

"Let's do it," urged his friend, laughing at Dick's reddening face, "Let's go on Sunday."

"Bloody hell," chortled Dick, "You're really not going to let up are you."

"No, I'm not," pressed the bookmaker, "I'll meet you at the bottom of your road at ten. And Dick?"

"Yeh?"

"I'm going to share something with you old pal."

The two men carried on drinking for a while, and chattered about their plans to cycle, catch fish and get themselves in shape. Oscar Renfrew was a firm believer in keeping trim and the suggestion to get out and about with Dick was a good-natured gesture at helping his friend to regain his former fit frame.

"Anyway," Dick slurred, starting to feel the full effect of the whisky, and wanting to change the subject, "Did Betty like her earrings?"

"She was over the moon," beamed Oscar, "Especially as I've promise her a matching bracelet for Christmas."

Dick sat upright. "I don't mean to pry Oscar," he sighed, "But that'll cost you a fortune."

"Oh, but she's worth it," smiled his friend, "Nothing's too much for my Betty."

"Have you got a secret stash?" joked Dick, wondering how on earth his friend could earn enough to fork out for diamonds at the drop of a hat.

"I own a betting shop!" chuckled Oscar Renfrew, standing up and pouring another drink.

"Oh, and I suppose you've got other secret talents as well have you," Dick sniffed.

"Come on that cycle ride and you'll find out," urged Oscar, "But not a word to anyone."

Dick chuckled and reached down to put his shoes back on, his friend was obviously more drunk than he'd first thought and that conclusion was a hint to end their partying.

"I'd best get on up the road," he said, "Give my regards to Betty."

"I'll see you bright and early Sunday morning," Oscar reminded him, "Get your bike cleaned!"

On Sunday, Dick was in a state of confusion. He'd hosed down his bicycle the day before and given it a good polish, even peddled a few yards around the back garden, but he wasn't at all convinced that he could manage a trip around the coast road. It must be ten years or more since I rode that thing, he pondered, pushing his black-framed racing bike to the front gate. He looked down at the small leather seat and sighed. Heaving his large backside up there would be a struggle, let alone sitting on such a little perch for a couple of hours. Still, he wasn't going to chicken out, if he could manage a steady ride once a week, perhaps it was a start to getting in shape. Besides, Oscar had got him curious now, mentioning his secret stash. Dick doubted that there was any real mystery, but he'd go along with it for a laugh.

Oscar Renfrew was waiting at the bottom of the cliff road as promised. He was dressed in light trousers and a crisp white shirt, the sleeves rolled up to his elbows. On the rear of his bicycle, he'd strapped a wicker basket from which a couple of fishing rods protruded. Seeing Dick opening his front gate, the bookmaker waved and set off up the hill to meet him.

Dick put one foot on the left pedal and heaved his leg over the bicycle frame, struggling to stay balanced. He knew fair well that Grace was watching from an upstairs window, and could just imagine her cackling laughter if he fell off before even making it to the main road. By some miraculous fluke, the large chap managed to steady himself just enough to keep the contraption going and clung tightly to the handlebars as he free-wheeled downhill. This was going to be a day to remember.

Oscar Renfrew stifled a laugh as Dick arrived next to him. Fair play, he thought, at least he's here and he's managing to stay upright.

"We'll take it steady," he assured Dick, mounting his own bicycle and peddling gently up the road, "Just follow me and shout if you need a rest."

"I'm ready for a rest now," muttered Dick, as he puffed away, trying desperately to keep up, 'What on earth have I let myself in for?'

Half an hour later, red faced and sweating profusely, Dick parked his racer next to Oscar's up against the coastal wall. It was a quite spot and there was no traffic on the road, so Dick presumed that this was where his friend planned to wander onto the beach to set up the fishing rods. However, jumping over the low rustic wall, Oscar left the basket behind and beckoned Dick to follow him over the rocks. The tide was out and no holidaymakers had yet discovered this fairly secluded spot.

It wasn't an easy task, heaving himself over the wall and then treading carefully on the slippery wet boulders, but Dick eventually managed to catch up with his companion as he was entering a small dark cave. Having no clue for the reasoning behind this expedition, Dick leaned back against the cold damp wall to catch his breath and looked around him. The cave was freezing, much colder than would normally be expected and pitch black, making visibility impossible. Suddenly Oscar switched on a flashlight.

"Bloody hell," Dick cursed, "Get that thing out of my eyes, and what are we doing in here?"

"Taking in the scenery," was the simple answer, "I can trust you to keep a secret, can't I Dick?"

Dick stifled a laugh, "Don't be daft Oscar, of course you can, we've been friends for years."

He could only make out the silhouette of his friend's body, but Oscar seemed to relax somewhat and turned to face the wall.

"Good, keeping your mouth shut just might earn you an added bonus now and again," Oscar announced, "Let's say in the form of a winning horse that you didn't actually bet on."

Dick Thomas was confused. He had no idea what his friend was rambling on about.

Oscar could see the other man's confusion and laughed, "Dodgy betting slips Dick! I'm going to pay you false winnings every Friday."

"Why would you do that?" Dick asked, more confused than ever.

Oscar didn't reply, but simply took a shovel from the back of the cave and began to dig. It took ten minutes for him to uncover the black plastic bin liner from its deep sandy grave and, when its contents were revealed, Dick stepped forward to inspect it.

"Look at this," Oscar beamed, dragging out a huge hessian sack, "Full to the brim with cash."

Dick read the words printed on the outside of the bag, "POST OF-FICE'.

"Why would you pay me to keep quiet about a mail bag?" he questioned, not understanding at all.

"To give me an alibi of course!" his friend exclaimed, "For the 8th of August last year. Just in case the coppers ever come snooping around."

Dick cast his mind back to almost a year before, "I'm still not with you....I..." but then suddenly it dawned on him. The newspaper headlines of 'The Great Train Robbery' had been implanted firmly in his mind.

Chapter Seven

Ned & Daisy Ashley

After three consecutive Sundays of fresh air and cycle rides with his friend, Dick Thomas was feeling quite proud of himself. He was certain that he'd lost a few pounds, although Grace had scoffed when he'd mentioned it, and he generally felt better for having taken some exercise. The first couple of outings had been the hardest, seeing Dick return home red-faced and saddle-sore but he was determined to continue his new found health kick, especially as it meant he could help Oscar to check on his hidden cash. The pair had chuckled like immature schoolboys as they'd discussed the bookmaker's fortune that first afternoon, but now that Dick had had time to get used to the idea of his friend having a secret, he went along with it. The added benefit of Dick now earning some extra money each week was too tempting to resist. Besides, he told himself, it was very unlikely that anybody would ever suspect the amiable bookie of anything.

In general, Dick was happy, and Grace had been a lot more relaxed lately too. She hadn't seemed to add any extra jobs to Dick's ever-growing list for a while and the chores that were on there were slowly but surely getting done. Most of the tasks were manageable ones, like mowing the lawn or cleaning the outside of the windows, but every now and again something major would need fixing and he was back to square one. A small matter that did need attending to however, was the despicable condition of both Dick's tyres and his bicycle seat. The rubber was wearing thin and the little padded seated was causing more discomfort than a ferret down the trousers, and Dick had been unable to sit comfortably in his armchair for a good while after his morning ride along the coast. Grace had, quite unkindly, commented that once her husband was aloft she was unable to see the seat at all, but Dick took no notice and resolved to get a new saddle fitted as a matter of urgency. The only place in town where such a service could be procured was 'Ashley's Garage' and so, one Monday morning, Dick set off to see what could be done.

Grace was busy dusting in the living room and secretly watched her husband from the window. He'd smartened himself up a great deal recently and had taken over a much more active role in the day to day running of the guest house. She couldn't yet call Dick an asset but he was certainly becoming useful. He was still wearing that silly cravat, but Grace was willing to overlook her husband's fashion faux pas, especially as her mother had insisted that it was the trendy thing for gentlemen to wear these days. Goodness, she thought, the 1960's had a lot to answer for. Still, some things never changed, she thought, contemplating how lovely it was to still see men coming for a day out at the seaside in their suits and ties. She dearly hoped that dressing up smartly for family outings would never go out of fashion.

Grace lifted up the cushions from each of the chairs and gave them a good shake. As she went to put them back into place, she couldn't help but notice a glint of something orange and white sticking out from down the side of the seat pad. She pushed her hand down to retrieve it and found herself staring at the Quentin Crisp book that had caused such a kerfuffle a few months before. So, Dick had taken to reading it again had he, she pondered, now what could be the reason for that?

Down at the local garage, Dick had found the proprietor prostrate under a car, his short stubby legs sticking out from just below the knee. Jazz music blared out from a portable radio in the workshop and a scruffy brown terrier bounced up and down at the office window, yapping frantically as Dick approached. He wheeled his bicycle to the far side wall and scrabbled to his knees to greet the mechanic.

"Alright Ned?" he huffed, craning his neck to see underneath the car, "How are you?"

Ned Ashley peddled his feet forwards on the low wooden trolley on which he lay and smiled up at Dick.

"Hey Dick, long time no see. Don't tell me you've finally bought a car?"

Dick looked towards the wall where his bike was parked and shook his head, "That's mine, over there."

The garage owner pulled himself to his feet and stood, all four feet eleven inches, on his tiptoes to see across the car bonnet to where Dick was motioning and started to laugh.

"Well, I never!" he chortled, "Dick Thomas riding a bike!"

Dick blushed and pretended to inspect his shoes while Ned Ashley got the laughter out of his system.

"Anyway," the little mechanic finally asked, "What can I do for you?"

Dick explained about the uncomfortable saddle and slowly deflating tyres while Ned inspected the racing bike at close quarters.

"She could do with a respray and a good oiling too," Ned tutted, firstly running his fat hands over the frame and then moving the pedals around to look at the chain, "I'm mighty busy today though."

"I don't need it until the weekend," Dick confirmed, hoping that he could have his bike back by Sunday.

"Oh, that's no problem," Ned smiled, "I'll have her as good as new by the end of the week."

"Grand," Dick beamed, "I appreciate that Ned."

"Let's have a brew while we discuss the cost," the garage owner offered, "I don't like to conduct my affairs out here on the forecourt."

Dick followed the short man through the cluttered workshop and into the office area, more than happy to part with his cash to get the bicycle smartened up. And if there was tea on the go, all the better!

Meanwhile, back at the guest house, distracted by the strange little book with the kangaroo cover, Grace had been sitting thinking. The book had reminded her of its owner Mr. Brown, and how he'd disappeared out into the world with not a word to anyone. Grace was far too much of a home bird to ever do anything like that but she wondered if a holiday overseas might be in order. Nowadays she was hearing of more and more people travelling to Europe and she quite fancied a trip to Italy or France. To be honest, even the Isle of Man would suffice in her eyes, but broaching the subject with Dick would be the difficult part.

And then something very strange happened.

As Grace sat looking at the paperback and dreaming of sunny beaches, the doorbell rang and on answering she was faced with two middle-aged men. One had a thick moustache and wore a brown trilby hat and dark overcoat, while the other had a sallow face and was more formally dressed in a navy suit. They held out cards, identifying themselves as policemen, and for a few seconds Grace was quite taken aback.

"Good morning madam," began the one with the moustache, "I wonder if we might trouble you for a few words. It's about a recent guest of yours," he flipped a little notepad open and read, "Josiah Wellings."

Grace's attention was immediately on full alert as she ushered the men into her sitting room.

"Tea?" she offered, wondering why on earth she suddenly felt nervous, "Or a cup of coffee?"

"No thank you," answered the man in the suit, "This shouldn't take long."

Grace perched precariously on the arm of a chair and smoothed down her dress as she waited for the policemen to explain. She felt the heat rising in her cheeks.

It seemed that Mr. Wellings had failed to return home after his coastal break at the Sandybank and his elderly mother had now registered him as a missing person. The police weren't too concerned, they said, as Mr. Wellings was a flighty character and had many friends up and down the country, but this was the first time he'd failed to let his mother know his whereabouts.

Grace trotted out into the hallway to fetch her leather-bound ledger and took a deep breath as she returned to the sitting room. She was aware of the radio playing in the kitchen and tutted at the irony of what was playing. Mr. Acker Bilk blasted out "Stranger On the Shore." There certainly couldn't have been anyone stranger than Josiah Wellings visiting these shores, she mused, pushing the door open, but what on earth did these policemen think she knew about it?

"Here we are," she explained, composing herself and running a forefinger down the page, "This is when he checked in, and then here, this is when he checked out."

Both men leaned forward to see and the one with the moustache jotted down something on his notepad.

They asked Grace a few questions about Josiah Wellings' activities during his stay, whether he made any phone calls and the last time she had physically seen him. After ten minutes, satisfied that there was nothing else to be learned from her, the policemen left Grace alone and strode down the path to their unmarked car. Grace watched them drive away and was just clicking the front door closed when a very significant thought struck her. She had failed to mention that their funny house guest had also been friends with Mr. Brown, another so-called missing person. Oh well, no doubt they would be back if it was significant, and if it wasn't, she hadn't burdened the busy detectives with unnecessary information. However, Grace couldn't help but wonder if their two single guests had been more than just friends.

Then later, as Grace recounted the policemen's visit to Dick over lunch, she couldn't help getting annoyed at his apparent lack of interest. It seemed that, apart from Josiah Wellings' mother, she was the only one who seemed bothered about the disappearance.

"Don't you think it's rather odd?" Grace asked, as she cleared away their plates, "I mean, the police seem to think that strange little man has just gone off somewhere."

"There's no telling what his sort get up to," grunted Dick, "Mr. Brown was another one."

Grace sighed as she considered this possibility, "I suppose I should have mentioned Mr. Brown to the police, shouldn't I? But, to be honest, I was so taken aback by them being here that I completely forgot all about him."

Dick shrugged, "Why would you say anything? Folks will think we only take in poofters at this rate?"

Grace rolled her eyes, "For goodness sake," she snapped, "It's none of our business what they get up to. Oh, and that reminds me, I found this down the side of your chair."

She pulled out 'All This and Bevin Too" from the kitchen drawer, and waited for her husband's reaction.

"And?" said Dick, looking confused, "What's that got to do with anything?"

"It seems this Quentin Crisp character is a very strange man," Grace sniffed, patting the book cover, "I asked Millie and she told me all about his odd ways. Josiah Wellings had nothing on him."

Dick picked up the book and then quickly set it down again, he was lost for words.

"Anyway, did Mr. Wellings leave a tip?" Grace asked, trying to pose the question as casually as possible.

"No, why would he?" shrugged Dick, starting to get annoyed with his wife's busy-bodying, "He paid his bill, we had a few farewell drinks and that was that."

"And he didn't add a couple of extra notes?" Grace prompted.

"No," sighed Dick, "He didn't. Look love, how many of our guests actually say 'Goodbye Mrs. Thomas, by the way your cooking was so fantastic that I want to give you an extra five pounds'?!"

"Well, it's very strange," Grace pushed gently, trying to ignore Dick's sarcasm, "I've noticed more money than usual in that tin lately."

"For goodness sake," huffed Dick, trying not to raise his voice, "I've been doing a few odd jobs for Oscar and he's been giving me some extra cash."

Grace nodded, "Of course you have Dick. That's why you never take your toolbox with you, don't spend more than a couple of hours down there and always wear that stupid cravat!"

"Hey now come on," Dick soothed, "Don't be like that, it's just between us blokes. I'm helping him out with something, that's all there is to it."

Grace turned her beady eyes on Dick and crossed her arms, "Oh, I bet. One of these days I'll get to the bottom of it and both of you will be sorry, very sorry indeed."

A couple of days later, on Friday afternoon, there was a knock at the back door. As Dick was sound asleep in his armchair, Grace stopped polishing cutlery and went to answer it.

"Hello Mrs. Thomas," beamed a red-haired youth of about ten or eleven, "Me Dad says that Mr. Thomas's bike is ready for him."

"Well, well, Brian Ashley," Grace smiled, recognising the young man immediately, "Come in lad. Would you like a glass of homemade lemonade?"

The boy nodded, "Yes please. That would be great."

Grace reached into the cabinet for a glass and began pouring out the drink from a pitcher.

"Here you go," she said, handing over the tumbler, "I'll just go and fetch Dick."

Brian stood sipping his lemonade as Grace rushed off to get her husband. He could hear a man's voice grumbling at being woken, followed by Mrs. Thomas tutting, and then both adults appeared at the kitchen door. Finishing his drink, the boy took his glass to the sink and stood smiling at the couple.

"Hello Mr. Thomas," he said, "Dad said your bike's as good as new now."

Dick thanked the boy and lifted his jacket from the coat hook, "I'll walk back with you and fetch it then."

Grace watched man and child leave the house and stood wondering at the boy's slender frame and shock of ginger hair. He looked nothing like his mother and father, who were both dark, short and chubby. Still, she knew that inherited looks and colouring could skip a generation, so perhaps the boy took after one of his grandparents. She shrugged and picked up a set of forks.

Meanwhile, Dick was having quite a chat with Brian Ashley as they strode down the road towards the garage. Brian was telling him all about wanting to become a mechanic just like his father and how, now that he was coming up to eleven, Ned had told his son that he could help out in the workshop at weekends, as long as his homework was finished first. Dick felt a tug at his heartstrings, how proud Ned must feel.

As Dick and Brian approached the garage forecourt, Ned Ashley came towards them, wiping his oily hands on a rag. He wore a woolly bobble hat and his overalls were filthy from lying under a motor car.

"Alright Dick?" the mechanic grinned, "There she is, up by the garden wall."

Dick followed Ned's gaze to where a gleaming bicycle leaned against the low brick wall that separated the garage premises from his family bungalow on the other side. It didn't look anything like the bike that he'd dropped off a few days ago. The frame had been given a new coat of paint, the spokes, chain and pedals sparkled and there, right on top of it all, was a brand new leather seat.

"Blimey," Dick gasped, "She looks brilliant."

Ned sauntered over towards the bike, closely followed by Dick and Brian.

"Our Brian did all the polishing," the little man explained, "And I managed to get you a deal on a saddle."

Dick took hold of the handlebars and touched the shiny black bicycle frame. He was delighted.

"I can't thank you enough," he managed at last, "Both of you, of course. She looks smashing."

Brian stood proudly next to his father, already towering over the short man, and folded his arms.

"I enjoyed working on that," he told Dick, "And your bike might go a bit faster now Mr. Thomas."

Dick chuckled, setting Ned Ashley off into a fit of laughter too.

Just then a light blue Triumph Herald pulled up on the forecourt with Daisy Ashley at the wheel. It took her a few seconds to heave her large body out of the driver's seat, and another few seconds to flip the seat forward to allow her twin daughters to climb out from the back. Audrey and Angela were pretty girls, with thick brown curls and chubby faces. They were dressed identically in lavender coloured frocks and short lacy ankle socks. At just six years old they were both boisterous and cheeky.

"Run along and play in the garden," their mother instructed, pulling a wicker shopping basket from the boot of the car, "And no teasing the cat."

Daisy Ashley was dressed in a pale blue cotton dress and navy cardigan. Despite her rotund figure, she was an attractive woman, with rosy cheeks and shoulder-length wavy hair. Her feet were squeezed into a pair of kitten heels which were obviously causing her discomfort as she walked.

"Hello love," Ned called, "Dick's just come to fetch his bicycle."

Suddenly realising that her husband had a customer, Daisy turned quickly around to greet Dick.

"Your girls are growing quickly," Dick commented, after the formalities were done with, "I hardly recognised them. They'll break some hearts when they grow up."

Both Ned and Daisy giggled, knowing full well that whichever brave lads married their daughters, they would most certainly have their hands full.

"I'd best settle my bill and get back on up the road," Dick commented after a few more minutes of idle chatter, "Grace will no doubt have a long list of chores waiting for me."

"Say hello to her," gushed Daisy, "We hardly see Grace, except in passing very briefly."

"Oh, I will," Dick assured her, "She's always got her hands full with the guests."

Dick felt a slight pang of guilt as he said those last words and realised that instead of standing here chattering he should, perhaps, get back up to the Sandybank and offer his help.

Having paid for Ned Ashley's services, a very reasonable sum considering all the work that had been done, Dick headed up the cliff road, pushing his gleaming bike gently along at his side. After a few steps, he turned and looked back at the family behind him. Ned and Daisy were deep in conversation outside the garage workshop, their dumpy twin daughters ran around in the bungalow garden and the lanky ginger-haired youth stood just inside the building sorting out his father's tools.

As Dick reached the cliff road, he could see an unfamiliar vehicle parked outside the gate of the guest house. It was very plain, a black Ford Anglia with no markings, just a splat of pigeon poop on the roof. As usual he entered through the back door and could hear a man's voice talking in another room. He went quietly into the hallway, tip-toeing gently, and listened.

"If you could just tell us what time Mr. Wellings left here, and which direction he was headed."

Dick could hear Grace telling whoever it was that she hadn't been here at the time and that it was her husband that had checked out their guest on the morning in question.

"And where is your husband now?" a different voice enquired, "Might we speak with him?"

Before waiting for Grace's reply, Dick turned on his heel and headed back out through the door. He had nothing to hide, in his eyes, but he always managed to make himself look guilty by getting tongue-tied, so he was far better off keeping out of the way. The potting shed looked like a good place to hide. He was half way across the lawn, when a gruff voice called out from behind him.

"Mr. Thomas? I wonder if we could have a word."

Dick stopped dead in his tracks and turned around. Two middle-aged men stood watching him from the patio. One of them had his arm raised and was beckoning Dick to come towards him. He's obviously scared of getting mud on his shoes, Dick thought to himself, typical pen pushers.

"Hello, there," Dick greeted them cheerfully, "Sorry, I didn't hear anyone arrive."

"You must have seen our car outside," one of the men said, "It's right outside the gate."

"Is it?" Dick chortled, "I must be in a world of my own today."

Both men introduced themselves as detectives and proceeded to ask Dick about his dealings with Josiah Wellings. Dick carefully recounted the morning of their guest's departure as best as he could.

One of the policemen, the taller of the two, made some notes in his book and smiled widely.

"Did you chat much with Mr. Wellings?" he asked casually.

"Chat?" repeated Dick Thomas, "Well, I suppose we had a few conversations about this and that."

"This and that?" the detective went on, "Several locals said they saw the two of you drinking in town together. Would that be correct?"

Dick coughed and looked sheepishly at his wife, "Only once," he admitted, "We just had a few pints."

"I see," the other man pondered, "That was all was it?"

"Yes," Dick confirmed, "That was definitely all."

"Thank you, Mr. Thomas," the other policeman said, "That will be all for now. Nice cravat by the way."

As the detectives headed down the garden path, Dick suddenly remembered the forged notes. He had forgotten to mention how their guest had duped him. Perhaps he should run after them and explain. He took two steps across the lawn and stopped. That would cause untold problems, he thought, as he hadn't told Grace about it. What with one thing and another, his winnings on the horses, going to the pub with Oscar, and then having changed the fake notes for real ones, Dick had got himself in a right pickle. He'd left it far too long to report the incident now, maybe things were best left alone. Besides, his winnings that day had more than covered for the lost income and nobody was any wiser.

It wasn't until about a week later that Dick walked down to the garage again. Grace had been baking and, as a token of appreciation for all Brian's hard work, she'd made half a dozen chocolate fairy cakes with buttercream icing for the Ashley children. Dick waited until four o'clock, when he knew the little ones would be home from school, before strolling down the hill with a cake tin in his hands. He'd been busy planting some runner beans that morning and Dick's back ached from bending over. However, knowing that if he settled into the chair for too long, Grace would find another task for her husband to attend to. A walk down to the garage would get him out from under her feet for an hour and, if he was lucky, he might get the offer of a cup of tea from Ned.

Sure enough, as he approached the garage, Dick spotted Brian's red hair gleaming in the sunlight. He had his back to the road and was busy washing a car with a bucket of soapy water and a chamois leather. Ned was on the telephone in the office and raised his hand in acknowledgement as Dick approached.

"Hello Mr. Thomas," Brian said cheerily, "Are you looking for my Dad?"

"It's alright son," Dick replied, "I can see he's busy. Anyway, it was you I came to see."

Brian Ashley put down the bucket and wrung out his cloth. He was dressed in a checked shirt and denim jeans, just like the American teenagers were wearing these days. "Really?" he said inquisitively.

"Aye," Dick confirmed, "I've brought cakes for you and your sisters."

He lifted the lid on the cake tin and showed the young boy what was inside.

"Wow! They look delicious!" the boy gushed excitedly, "And there's two each!"

"Maybe best to wait until after you tea though eh?" Dick laughed, seeing how Brian's eyes had lit up.

"What's all this then?" called Ned Ashley, having finished his call and coming out to see the visitor.

Dick explained his purpose for calling and passed the cakes to Brian.

"Really, you shouldn't have," enthused Ned, now shaking Dick's hand, "That's very kind of you."

"Make sure you share with your sisters won't you?" he called to his son, as Brian raced across the lawn with the cake tin carefully held aloft.

"I will Dad," the boy shouted, glancing back over his shoulder.

"He's a grand lad," Dick commented as he watched the boy clamber up the steps to the porch, his long legs managing two at a time, "I'll bet those girls of yours run rings around him."

Ned laughed, "They certainly do. Poor lad spends hours having to play pretend tea parties or sit in their make believe classrooms while they try to teach him."

Dick chuckled and waited for the mechanic to go on. Strangely Ned changed the subject.

"I saw the coppers were up at yours last week."

Dick bit the skin around his thumbnail and raised an eyebrow, "Oh aye, how do you know that then?"

"They called here for petrol," Ned answered, "Could tell they were the fuzz a mile away."

Dick coughed. "One of our guests has done a moonlight flit."

"Oh, not that poncy looking fellow that came in the pub?"

Dick shuffled his feet and nodded, "Aye, Josiah Wellings his name was."

"I hope he paid you first!" Ned chortled, thrusting his hands into his overall pockets.

Dick nodded sheepishly, "Of course! Nobody pulls the wool over my eyes!"

"Ha, ha, good lad," Ned smiled, clapping Dick on the back, "How about a brew while you're here?"

Dick stood passing the time of day with Ned for a good twenty minutes before Daisy Ashley ushered the twins outside to thank him for the fairy cakes. He could see from the gooey chocolate mess around the little girl's mouths that their mother had failed to keep the treats from them for very long. Each girl had sticky fingers and dark crumbs stuck to the front of their lemon-coloured dresses.

"Thank you for the cakes Mr. Thomas," Audrey and Angela chimed at exactly the same time grinning widely.

"Yes, thank you very much," added Brian, following up the rear, "I'm saving mine for later."

"Have you done your homework lad?" Ned asked his son, playfully nudging him with his elbow.

"Yes Dad," laughed the boy, "I did it as soon as I got home."

"Good on you," grinned the mechanic, "You'll have time to wash another car before bedtime."

"No problem," Brian countered, smiling proudly at his father, "I might even do two."

Dick beamed. Bless them, he thought, what lovely children.

"Come on, inside and wash your hands for tea," Daisy clucked, "And thank Grace for us will you Dick?"

Dick nodded and watched all three children race back up to the bungalow. Ned was watching them too. There never was a prouder man, Dick thought, noticing how the garage owner's mouth had creased at the corners and a definite twinkle glinted in his eye.

"Lovely manners, your children," Dick commented when they'd disappeared from view,

Ned Ashley turned around, looking as pleased as punch, "They're great aren't they?"

"Different as chalk and cheese though, Brian and the girls," commented Dick.

It was as though an arrow had hit the mechanic through the heart, visibly flinching, and he sucked in his breath before answering.

"Well, it's only to be expected," he whispered, looking around to make sure nobody else was in earshot.

"What do you mean?" asked Dick, not registering that there was something wrong in the little man's tone.

"Well, look at Brian's mop of red hair," he began, "He looks just like the milkman."

Dick gave a nervous laugh and wrung his hands together. "Ha, the milkman, that's a good one."

That was something that his own mother and father had joked about when Dick and his siblings misbehaved. Or had they said the coalman, he pondered.

Ned tilted his head on one side to avoid the glare of the sun as he looked at Dick.

"You don't know do you?" he asked nervously.

"Know what?"

"Our Brian really is the milkman's," Ned continued, wiping his brow with a greyish handkerchief, "Stevie Robins from the dairy to be exact. He, erm, offered to help us out when Daisy and I couldn't get pregnant years ago. Luckily it only took a couple of goes. Thought I had no swimmers see, but then we had the twins later on so it turned out I was alright after all."

'You mean, Stevie and Daisy actually had to....," Dick started, unable to believe his ears.

"Oh aye," nodded the mechanic, "We didn't see any other way."

Dick formed a big round 'O' with his mouth and sat down on the wall with a thud.

Chapter Eight

Hilda Price

It was Friday morning. Dick had gone to fetch his newspaper and Grace was busy in the kitchen making fruit scones for the weekend. The guest house was busy, having only one single room free, indicating that the holiday season was in full swing. The weeks were passing quickly for Grace, who was in her element organising, cleaning, hosting and cooking. She had to admit that Dick had been pulling his weight too, keeping the gardens neat, taking out rubbish and going down to the market for supplies as and when necessary. He'd even added another two concrete slabs to the patio area, although his wife had just about given up hope of them being able to use it this summer.

As Grace sifted flour and rubbed in butter, she heard the familiar tread of Robbie Powell's boots on the path outside. She called to him to come straight in, as her hands were too sticky with dough to try opening the back door. Robbie stepped inside and grinned.

"Hello love," Grace smiled back at the young fisherman, "You'll have to put the kettle on yourself if you want a brew." She raised her floury hands to show him she was indisposed.

"No worries," Robbie shrugged, reaching for the kettle and taking it to the sink, "What sweet treats have you got for your guests today then?"

Grace explained that her scones were for afternoon tea on Saturday, "Folks are usually hungry after a day on the beach," she added, "And if they're not, they can take them in a picnic basket the next day."

Robbie took two cups out of the kitchen cupboard and then turned his attention to the wicker basket that he'd brought in with him. Taking out a large parcel, he showed Grace the contents.

"I've got a lovely piece of hake for you today, and Dad's sent half a dozen kippers, smoked them himself."

"Oh my word," cooed Grace, looking impressed, "Those will be gone in no time, most of our older gentlemen guests prefer kippers to a full English breakfast."

"I hope you serve them with bread and butter," Robbie prompted.

"Of course!" Grace answered, pretending to be shocked, "Wouldn't dream of any other way."

As Grace was still in the process of finishing her dough, Robbie put the parcel of fish into the cold store and then came back to finish making the tea. He enjoyed his Friday morning chats with Grace, as she'd quite often got new ideas for storylines in his romance novels, which were now starting to pay off. He also liked that fact that she usually sent him home with slices of cake to satisfy his father's sweet tooth.

After twenty minutes of idle chatter, about books, guests and gossip in town, Grace took her scones out of the oven to cool. Robbie twitched his nose in appreciation.

"They smell delicious," he hinted, hoping that Grace would let him try one.

"Get a plate then," she sighed, smiling as she said it, "The butter's on the table."

Robbie Powell got up quickly and darted forward to the dresser where Grace displayed her china plates. Suddenly, slipping on a small puddle of water that had leaked from his basket, the young man lurched sideways and ended up flat on the floor. He lay still for a few seconds and then blinked up at Grace, who had rushed to his side.

"Goodness me," she fussed, "Are you alright?"

Robbie nodded and tried to get up. There was nothing broken, of that he was sure, but his back ached terribly. It must be badly bruised, Robbie supposed. He took a deep breath and tried to stand up.

Just as the young man was pulling himself to his feet, with Grace's help, Dick returned home. Seeing that the fisherman was in obvious pain, Dick rushed to his aid and succeeded in getting him onto a chair.

"Shall I call Dr. Grimes?" Grace asked, genuinely concerned, "You might have pulled something."

Robbie shook his head, "No, really, I'll be alright. Maybe I'll just rest this afternoon though."

"Aye, good idea," agreed Dick, speaking for the first time, "I'll help you home."

"Thanks Mr. Thomas," Robbie replied, wincing slightly as he tried to straighten himself up. Suddenly he had a thought and sighed heavily, "I can't go home, I've still got one more delivery to make."

"You're going nowhere but bed," Grace ordered, "Who's is the last delivery? Maybe Dick can take it?"

Robbie looked sheepishly up at Dick, he didn't like having to burden other people with things but he really had no other choice, as his back was really painful.

"It's for Hilda Price," he finally said, "The lady in the grey stone house next to the school."

"Oh, in the opposite direction to your house," Dick muttered, rolling his eyes dramatically at Grace.

"No worries," Grace said kindly, glancing quickly up at the clock, "I've got time to take it for you."

"That's settled then," Dick nodded, "Come on lad, let me help you get home to bed."

Grace quickly tidied up the tea cups as Dick and Robbie disappeared down the path, it wouldn't take her long to walk to the house that Robbie had mentioned and, after all, the fresh air would do her good.

It has to be said that Grace didn't know Hilda Price very well at all, apart from having said 'hello' in passing at the market or occasionally seeing the tall, smart woman rushing towards the chapel on Sundays where she was the organist. Grace had heard that the woman led a very sedentary life, reading her vast collection of books, teaching piano at her home to anyone who wanted to learn, and hammering out hymns on the hundred year old organ at the weekends. Still, none of that mattered to Grace, she had fish to deliver and deliver it she would.

Scooping up the last remaining parcel from Robbie's wicker basket, Grace dropped it into her blue string bag and set off down the road. She hummed a tune as she walked and enjoyed the feel of the warm sunshine on her face. As she looked right, towards the sea, Grace could see children having donkey rides on the beach, a cockle seller plying his trade from a mobile cart and families building sandcastles with their plastic buckets and spades. Grace could never imagine living anywhere else, the seaside town had been a part of her life for so long that it would be unthinkable to even contemplate moving. As she walked, Grace turned her thoughts once again to holidays. Maybe she didn't need to go abroad, she mused, after all wasn't one seaside town much the same as any other?

As she turned a corner, the local school came into view. Grace could hear the children playing happily before she could see them, the chanting songs of girls skipping, the shouts of boys playing with a ball and the shrill piercing sound of a teacher's whistle as they gave a warning when things became too boisterous. And there, imposing and dark, separated by a high privet hedge, was the grey stone house belonging to Hilda Price. It was hard not to notice the very grand, sleek car parked outside, and Grace was sure that she recognised it as a Rolls Royce. Her curiosity piqued, Grace quickened her step and crossed over the road until she was standing on the pavement next to the motor vehicle.

As she briefly stopped to check her appearance in the reflection of the tinted windows, Grace heard the door of the house open behind her. A very familiar looking gentleman stepped out and, immediately he did so, a man in a chauffeur's uniform appeared from the side of the house. Ooh, the driver must have been waiting outside, Grace contemplated, I wonder why not wait in the car? Just then a woman appeared.

She was dressed in a tightly fitting pencil skirt and cashmere sweater, obviously not an outfit that she'd picked up at Woolworth's.

"Good bye darling," Hilda Price whispered sweetly, "You will try to come again soon won't you?"

Grace saw the man nod, say something in the woman's ear, pull a peaked cap down low over his brow and then turn around to leave. He suddenly noticed Grace standing at the roadside watching and coughed.

Grace smiled widely and muttered a faint greeting but in a flash both the man and his driver had hurried past her and jumped in the car. Seconds later they were gone. Grace stood perfectly still for a few seconds, trying to recall where she had seen the gentleman before.

"Can I help you?" Hilda Price called from the doorstep.

"Oh, yes, I'm sorry," Grace chirped, embarrassed that she had seemed like a nosey passer-by, "I've brought your fish from Robbie."

Hilda Price looked slightly confused and waited for Grace to explain, which she did, in great detail.

"Oh, I see," the other woman smiled, "How very kind of you. Please do come in."

Grace couldn't help noticing the perfect way in which Hilda Price pronounced her words, almost without accent and felt slightly humbled as she stepped inside. The hallway was very dark, painted entirely in a dark teal colour and, rather surprisingly, the walls were adorned with sketches of nude figures hung in heavy gilt frames. Grace stamped her feet on the doormat and followed the house owner down the long corridor to a room at the back of the house. As she watched the woman gliding along like a prima ballerina, Grace became aware of her own slouching figure and straightened herself up in an attempt to feign elegance.

'Here we are," Hilda Price announced, opening the door to an enormous oak kitchen, "Can I get you anything? A glass of water? A cup of tea?"

Grace shook her head slowly, looking around in awe as she spoke, "No thank you dear."

Hilda Price politely relieved Grace of the parcel of fish and gently unwrapped it.

"This is for my babies," she announced proudly, "Let me show you."

Grace stood with her hands in front of her, waiting for the woman to continue, but instead she opened a side door and called to someone or something on the other side.

"Marmalade, Ginger, Sooty."

The first of Hilda Price's trio to arrive was an enormous tortoiseshell cat with orange eyes and thick dense fur, it was closely followed by a slim but well-groomed ginger tom cat. The last feline to arrive was black and long-haired with the only other colour being its shiny emerald eyes. All three cats looked at Grace.

"Little rascals have been out pestering the birds no doubt," Hilda Price smiled, affectionately stroking each cat in turn as they rubbed against her legs, "Do you like cats Mrs. Thomas?"

"Well, erm, to tell the truth I've not really had much to do with them," Grace confessed, feeling slightly embarrassed by her answer, "I must say, your cats are very handsome."

Hilda Price gave a little laugh and turned to face her visitor, "How much do I owe for the fish?"

"Oh, I have no idea," Grace said truthfully, "You'd best just sort it out with Robbie next week."

The other woman nodded and took a pan from the cupboard, "I'd better poach this," she said, pointing at the large piece of cod that lay forlornly in its paper wrapper, "These kitties look hungry."

Grace didn't know what to say. Was this woman really going to feed her cats a piece of fresh cod? The idea seemed unthinkable, what was wrong with pet food?

"I'd better be on my way," she eventually murmured, "I have such a lot to do up at the house."

"Of course, let me show you out," Hilda Price offered, "And thank you again Mrs. Thomas."

The two women walked to the front door in silence, Grace in front, taking in the beautiful parquet flooring and glass beaded lampshade hanging above her head, and Hilda Price walking slowly behind looking at the rather frumpy figure of the guest house owner.

"Goodbye Mrs. Thomas," the house owner began, "It was lovely to see you."

Grace hitched her handbag up into the crook of her arm, "You too Mrs. Price."

"It's Miss," the lady corrected, "I've never been married."

"Oh, right you are," noted Grace, stepping onto the path and preparing to leave.

"Mrs. Thomas?" added Hilda Price, beckoning Grace back towards her, "The visitor that you saw earlier?"

Grace pricked up her ears and nodded.

"Well, you didn't see him, alright?"

Grace opened her mouth to contradict the other woman but changed her mind. Oh, so it was some illicit affair was it, she thought, probably with a married man!

Back at the guest house, Dick was in the kitchen with the newspaper spread out on the table. He was circling his horses with a thick marker pen.

"Alright love?" he asked, looking up as Grace closed the back door, "How was Mrs. Price?"

"Oh, you mean Miss. Price." she replied sternly, following up the remark with a full disclosure on what she had seen on arrival at the grey house.

"Was it anyone we might know?" Dick inquired, genuinely quite intrigued by the revelation.

"Well, that's the funny thing," confirmed his wife, "I've definitely seen that gentleman somewhere before, his face looked so familiar, but I don't think he lives around here."

Dick sniffed, "Never mind love, you'll remember at some point, you always do."

A week went by, in a flurry of lively house guests, delicious meals and lots of cleaning. Now fully recovered from his injury, Robbie Powell had dropped off the Friday fish delivery and was on his way back down the path when Grace suddenly remembered that she wanted to tell him something.

"Robbie," she called from the open kitchen door, "I forgot to mention, I told Miss. Price to sort out the money for the fish with you personally."

The young man, raised his basket and shouted, "It's alright, I've got another delivery for her here, so I'll sort it out with Mrs. Price today."

"She's a Miss," Grace blurted out, not really meaning to.

Robbie started walking back up the path to where Grace was now standing, his face full of confusion.

"Oh" he remarked, "I just presumed she had a husband. I often see a car parked outside her house."

Grace folded her arms, seeing that Robbie was interested in what she knew, "It belongs to her gentleman friend," she babbled, "But don't tell anyone, I'm sworn to secrecy."

Robbie chuckled, women, they can't resist a bit of juicy gossip, he thought.

"Well, you didn't tell me," he winked cheekily, "I know nothing!"

Grace nodded, satisfied that her scandal-mongering would go no further. Well, it was only Robbie.

A few days later, with four guests checked out and another three due the following day, Grace was busily pulling sheets off the beds and replacing them with fresh ones. Wanting to help, Dick ambled upstairs and offered to carry the laundry downstairs to the twin tub.

"Thank you," Grace puffed, "If you take them down, I'll switch the machine on when I've finished here."

"No worries," Dick assured her, "I can manage, I've just about got the hang of it now."

Grace smiled warmly and plumped up a pillow, "I'll get this room ready first, Mr. and Mrs. Williams arrive in the morning, and then Arthur Baxter tomorrow afternoon."

The moment that the gentleman's name fell from her lips, Grace gasped in horror, "Oh my goodness Dick! Mr. Baxter is a vegetarian!"

"Well, I can always pop down to the market to get some vegetables and stuff," Dick assured her, "Do you know what you need?"

"No," huffed Grace, "I haven't even thought about it. I tell you what, I'll finish up here and then I'll go to the market. If I can see what's fresh and colourful, it might give me some inspiration."

"Right you are," her husband agreed, gathering up the dirty sheets in his arms, "I'll put these on then."

By mid-day, Grace had set off down the hill with her little string bag, leaving Dick snoozing in his chair. It was a lovely sunny day and, dressed in a pale pink shift with her trusty Mary-Jane shoes, Grace could see that the freckles on her arms had become more prominent in the sun. She really did love this time of year, with a busy guest house, laughter emanating from the beach and the beautiful sheen that seemed to glimmer from the surface of the sea. No, she wouldn't suggest a holiday this year, home was exactly where she wanted to be, at least for the rest of the year.

Passing the harbour wall, Grace paused for a moment and looked around for Robbie Powell, he was usually repairing nets or cleaning barnacles off the hull around this time but there was no sign of him or his fishing boat today. Grace carried on along the pavement, passing the hairdressing salon, the bookmaker's and the sweet shop. She couldn't help smiling faintly as her thoughts once again turned to old Mrs. Cole and her handsome young men. Whoever would have thought it!

Arriving at the indoor market hall, Grace glanced around to see if there was anyone she knew. In fact, it was a busy morning, and she was greeted several times by people with whom she was well acquainted. Millie Meacham was there, looking very sophisticated in a striped Breton t-shirt and navy shorts, Daisy Ashley was busily filling a basket with strawberries and apples, and even Grace's own mother was busily selecting vegetables from the abundance of produce on display.

Therefore, it took Grace a good fifteen minutes to finish saying 'Good Morning' to everyone before she could even contemplate choosing her goods. Still, it was lovely to get out and about.

After briefly asking her mother's advice on what to prepare for Mr. Baxter, Grace headed to the fruit and vegetable stall to buy the components for a fresh salad and a cauliflower, with which she would serve a creamy cheese sauce. Their vegetarian guest would be staying for a whole week, Grace reminded herself, so she dearly hoped that she could come up with a few more inspiring meals over the next few days. For her own mind, Grace couldn't imagine a life without meat or fish, it was simply unheard of.

As she selected some big juicy plum tomatoes, Grace felt a shoulder rub against her own as the person next to her reached across to pick some too. The hand that gathered the fruit wore a very expensive gold watch and had immaculately painted red fingernails. She looked upwards to see the owner's face.

"Hello Mrs. Thomas," smirked Hilda Price, her eyes smouldering like a cat, "How are you?"

"Very well, thank you," Grace responded cheerfully, "And you? Are your furry babies well?"

Hilda Price laughed, causing her full-skirted dress to swish around her hips, "Oh, yes, those naughty pussycats are just fine."

Grace nodded towards the tomatoes in the tall woman's hand, "They look lovely and juicy don't they?"

"They certainly do," conceded Miss. Price, "I'm a vegetarian, so I get through a great deal of salad stuff every week. Although I still have to buy fish for my little darlings."

Grace stifled a chuckle and stood taking in the information. It suddenly dawned on her that she could ask Miss. Price for advice on what to feed Mr. Baxter.

Quickly explaining her dilemma, Grace confessed to not really having had to cater for a vegetarian before and she didn't mind admitting that she found the task quite daunting. Hilda Price listened intently.

"I tell you what," she eventually said, taking Grace by the arm, "Come back to my house and I'll let you have one of my vegetarian cookery books."

Grace blinked, "Oh no, I simply couldn't trouble you," she faltered.

"Nonsense," Hilda Price announced briskly, "We can be there in ten minutes. I have plenty of books, so one less won't make a difference, and you will have one very satisfied vegetarian guest."

Grace grinned, "Why thank you Mrs, erm, Miss. Price! That would be wonderful."

"Hilda, please," the elegant woman coaxed, "Come on then, what are we waiting for?"

Arriving at the very imposing grey house, Hilda Price once again led her visitor into the kitchen. It was immaculate, as it was last time, except for a single wine glass turned upside down on the draining board.

"Please sit down," Miss. Price said, indicating for Grace to take a seat at the long wooden table that dominated the centre of the room, "I'll get a few books for you to choose from."

"This really is very kind," Grace started to say, but her words were met with dismissal, as the other lady shook her head and headed for a shelf lined with cookery volumes. Quickly thumbing through, and brushing past her favourite ones, Hilda Price selected four thick books and brought them to the table.

"I'll make us a coffee while you decide which one will suit your purpose," she told Grace, her voice soft but still bearing an aloofness that was easy to detect, "Do you take milk and sugar?"

Grace answered in the affirmative and started flicking through the heavy cookery books with their detailed descriptions and glossy photographs. They must be very expensive books, she thought, rubbing a hand across the shiny surface.

"Do you see anything suitable?" Hilda Price asked, coming to stand at Grace's shoulder as she sat hunched over the table. She picked up one of the books, "How about making a nut roast?"

Grace looked down at the page that the woman was indicating and her eyes lit up. Not only did it look filling but judging by the ingredients it wouldn't cost a lot to make either.

"Gosh, that looks amazing," she admitted, "I think Mr. Baxter would be happy with that."

"That's settled then," Hilda Price declared, "That's the book that you shall have."

After preparing the coffee in a pair of transparent glass cups, and then placing them on matching saucers, the house owner came to seat herself opposite Grace at the huge wooden table. She smiled, watching her guest closely.

"Are you happy Mrs. Thomas?" she asked slowly and deliberately.

Grace was quite taken aback by the question, it wasn't the type of thing that she got asked every day.

"Why, yes, of course," she began, "Well, most days anyway."

"That's good," Miss. Price commented, "You must have a very loving husband."

Grace laughed, a little embarrassed at the other woman being so blunt. "He's a good man," she finally said, "He's got his faults, but he's a good man at heart."

Hilda Price sat watching the changing expressions on the landlady's face as she spoke, she could see that there was more going on under the surface of the Thomas's relationship, but she chose not to pry.

The tortoiseshell cat, who unbeknown to Grace had been curled up on the seat of another chair under the table, suddenly poked its head up and gave a loud yawn.

Both women giggled, breaking the ice between them.

"I guess Marmalade is bored with our idle chatter," Hilda Price joked, "Aren't you sweetie?"

She ruffled the huge cat under the chin and kissed one of its fat furry cheeks.

Grace flinched slightly, she would never dream of doing that to a cat, her own or otherwise.

"I'd better go home and make a start on this nut roast," she mused, finishing her last sip of coffee.

"Here, let me put the book into a bag for you," her host offered, quickly pulling a cotton tote bag from a cupboard, "It will make it easier to carry. You already have all your vegetables."

Grace looked down at her blue string bag, blushing slightly, why had she chosen to use this tatty old thing? Miss. Price must think her so unrefined.

"Thank you, I'll return it of course," she said politely, taking the bag in her hands.

"Oh no, don't be silly," joked Hilda Price, "I have literally hundreds of those things."

"Well, thank you," Grace smiled, "And for the cookery book, it's really very kind of you."

As they trotted down the hallway, Grace's Mary Jane shoes squeaking on the polished floor and Hilda Price's kitten heels clicking as she followed, the silhouette of a man could be seen walking towards the frosted front door and suddenly the house owner seemed to panic.

"Oh my goodness," she gasped, "Mrs. Thomas, would you mind going out through the back door? Oh no, never mind, it's too late now. Oh, gosh, how very awkward."

"It's alright dear," Grace clucked trying to soothe the woman, "Your secret's safe with me."

"Really?" Hilda Price countered, starting to panic even more, "Oh, Mrs. Thomas you really mustn't say a word to anyone, ever. Please, you do understand the repercussions don't you?"

Grace nodded and thought the performance to be very extreme, although she made a promise and continued to the front door where the gentleman on the other side was now ringing the doorbell.

Turning the heavy brass doorknob, Grace swung the door inwards and stood looking at the man who was waiting patiently to enter. However, on realising that it was not, in fact, the home owner who had answered the door, the man looked extremely startled and suddenly hid his face in his overcoat lapel. The glimpse that Grace had seen of him was just enough to know that it was the man who had been visiting Miss. Price last time she was here. Grace was surprised too, she had never received such a reaction by simply opening a door before.

"Hello," she offered meekly, "I didn't mean to shock you."

The man glanced up, only allowing his eyes to be seen. He nodded and muttered something incomprehensible, waiting for Grace to pass through the doorway, which she quickly did.

"Goodbye then," she mumbled, looking back at Hilda Price.

Unfortunately the woman was too busy bustling her guest inside to take much notice of Grace's departure and she closed the door without any further hesitation.

Grace shook her head in disbelief, what a carry on, she thought. It was then that she realised someone else was watching her from the corner of the house. It was the chauffeur.

He coughed, and narrowed his eyes, watching Grace continue on her way, which she did, briefly taking a sidelong glance at the Rolls Royce parked at the kerb. She walked quickly away, one bag held tightly in each hand, still confused about all the commotion of the new arrival. Even if the man was married, did the situation really need to be so cloak and dagger theatrical, she asked herself.

As Grace unloaded the vegetables and put Hilda Price's cookery book on the table to look through later, Dick came lumbering into the kitchen.

"You've been gone a long time love," he commented, looking genuinely concerned, "I was just about to send out a search party."

Grace explained about the recipe ideas and the strange incident in which she had just been involved.

"Oh, don't worry your pretty little head about Miss. Price and her fancy man," Dick soothed, "It's none of our business, no doubt his wife will find out sooner or later."

"Do you have any idea who he is?" Grace quizzed, hoping that her husband would say that he did.

"Nope," confessed Dick, "Can't say I do."

Grace sidled over to the kettle. She needed another drink to settle her nerves.

"Anyway," continued Dick, reaching across to where he'd put a glossy magazine on top of the bread bin, "I saved this for you, thought you might like it."

Grace glanced briefly over to where Dick was holding a shiny pull-out that spread across two pages.

"What is it?" she asked, still only half-heartedly interested in anything other than Hilda Price.

"It's a full-page spread of the Royal family," Dick grinned, "Look at that, three generations all standing proud for the official photographer. Think it was taken for the Queen's birthday."

Grace smiled and glanced over to where her husband was holding up the picture for her to see.

Something caught her eye suddenly, and she quickly stepped over to get a closer look.

There standing right behind the Queen's shoulder was the Prince. Oh my goodness, she gasped, unable to speak. Those broad shoulders, that dark moustache and hazelnut eyes.

Not only did he look familiar, but Grace had been face to face with him that very afternoon.

Chapter Nine

Elliot Moss

One thing that Dick particularly enjoyed about his morning stroll to the newsagents in the summer months was the sight of children having donkey rides on the beach. Their little faces lit up in delight as they were hoisted into the saddle and, when the ride was over, they would plead with their parents to let them go again. On this particular morning, as Dick walked slowly down the hill, he could see a queue of happy faces all waiting to ride 'Elvis', 'Pandora', 'Annabel', 'Sooty' and 'Jerry'.

Dick knew Elliot Moss, the proprietor of the donkey rides business, very well. In fact, in their younger days, he and Grace had played bridge with Elliot and his wife. Sadly, their card playing evenings had come to an end quite abruptly when Betty Moss had become seriously ill. When she died, Elliot had become quite withdrawn and stopped going out altogether, Dick rarely even saw his old friend in the pub these days. The Thomas's hadn't been able to attend poor Betty's funeral, as Elliot had insisted upon no fuss, saying something about taking her body three hundred miles away, up north to her hometown. He hadn't even wanted wreaths or flowers from his friends to lay at her grave, but everyone had sent cards of sympathy to the young widower. Poor Elliot was a very private man, and the seaside folk allowed him the space to grieve in peace. Still, the whole town had been in mourning for Betty Moss and there had been a huge turnout at the memorial service. Beautiful woman she was too, Dick reflected, conjuring up a picture of Betty Moss in his mind.

As he neared the coastal wall, Dick could see Elliot more clearly, with his shirt sleeves rolled up and leather braces holding up his work trousers, which were extremely baggy due to all the weight he'd lost over the years. He wore a brown flat cap to keep the sun out of his eyes and to stop the rays burning his scalp, which had become more exposed recently from loss of hair. Poor chap, Dick thought to himself, maybe we should invite him up for dinner one night.

Just then Elliot Moss happened to look up, as he led 'Elvis' and his passenger along the sand, and on seeing Dick he grinned and waved his hand. Dick waved back and stuck his thumb up, resolving to speak to Grace about his old friend as soon as he got home.

As it happened, Grace was run off her feet with guests that day, some checking out in the morning and others checking in during the afternoon. The house was a torrent of hoovering, sheet-washing and bed-making, with Grace running up and downstairs and tutting all the while. Dick had offered to help, but as usual he had been told that everything was under control, despite his wife's wrinkled brow and heavy tread on the staircase. By four o'clock things had settled down, beds were made, guests had checked in, depositing their suitcases and heading straight out to the beach, and the washing-line was one long row of brilliant white sheets blowing in the breeze.

It was at that point that Grace sat down for a cup of tea and a couple of digestive biscuits.

"I saw Elliot Moss this morning", Dick commented as he poured the tea from the pot into a china cup for his wife, "He's looking old these days."

"Mmmm, well, I suppose he's a few years older than us isn't he?" Grace muttered, not really taking an interest, "He must be nearly fifty."

"He's forty-eight," Dick corrected her, "But looking more like sixty-eight."

"Well, I don't suppose he feels like taking care of himself after Betty," Grace replied, looking up at Dick for the first time since she'd sat down at the kitchen table.

"I was wondering if we should invite him to dinner one night," Dick casually hinted, "I mean, it would be nice to catch up with him and he doesn't get out much."

Grace huffed and rolled her eyes, "Like I haven't got enough to do around here."

"He was your friend too," Dick pointed out, "And we've neglected a lot of our friends lately."

Grace stiffened and sipped her tea, thinking.

"Alright," she finally answered, "Invite him round for dinner on Friday night."

"Only if you're sure now," Dick soothed, not wanting to start an argument.

"I'm sure," Grace nodded, "You're right, Elliot and Betty were good friends of ours."

That evening as Dick began his second stroll of the day, towards the Miner's Arms, he took a slight detour to the long row of red brick terraced houses that stood along the coastal road, where it snaked eastwards towards the next town. He passed the houses every Sunday on his bicycle rides with Oscar but, as Elliot was busy on the beach with his donkeys, it never occurred to him to call in. Besides, after the exertion of an hour sitting on that small leather saddle, Dick was always eager to get home and put his feet up. Today though, things were different. He was determined to convince his friend to join them for a meal and also to rekindle the friendship of days gone by.

As he knocked at Elliot Moss's door, Dick took in the peeling paint on the window ledges and overgrown front garden. Perhaps he could also offer his help in getting the house tidied up, he thought, it certainly looked as though Elliot could do with some assistance. Still, it was only to be expected, Betty had been a keen gardener and had always been known as a wonderful housewife.

Elliot Moss answered the door on Dick's second knock. He was surprised to receive a visitor at any time of the day or night, but seeing his old friend standing there was quite unexpected.

"Hello Dick," he grinned, opening the door just a fraction, "What brings you here? Are you lost?"

Dick gave a short laugh but the embarrassment of not visiting for so long was clearly visible in his red cheeks and lack of eye contact.

"Aye, it's certainly been a while," he finally managed to say, "How are you keeping Elliot?"

"I'm alright," the other man admitted after a pause, "Well, don't just stand there, come on in."

He opened the door wide, and gestured for Dick to enter.

"Take a seat," Elliot smiled, indicating a comfy chair, "I'll get us a cold beer."

"That'll be smashing," Dick replied, sinking down into the huge chair, and looking around.

The room was exactly the same as he'd remembered it from years before, except the carpet was a bit threadbare and the arms of the chairs were showing signs of wear and tear. There were photos of Betty covering the sideboard and her collection of owl figurines were still displayed along the mantle-piece. A strange musty smell permeated the air, not enough to take Dick's breath away, but definitely the odour of something old and decayed. He wondered if the homeowner had noticed it himself.

"Here we are," Elliot Moss announced, passing a bottle of beer and an empty glass to Dick, "Just like old times eh? Bit of a surprise seeing you here though."

Dick smiled meekly, "Aye, and it's been far too long. I'm sorry for that Elliot, I really am."

His friend settled back onto the sofa and shrugged, "Well, it's my fault too, I'm always busy."

The two men sipped their beer in silence for a few minutes, both feeling awkward and unable to think of something appropriate to say. It was Dick who finally restarted the conversation.

"Grace and I were wondering if you'd like to come for dinner on Friday night."

Elliot Moss was taken aback and sat blinking at Dick from across the room.

"I guess it'll be fish then?" he finally asked, a cheeky smirk playing on his lips.

Dick chuckled, "Aye, always bloody fish on a Friday." The ice between them had finally been broken.

When Friday came around, Elliot Moss arrived right on time. Dick had been looking out for him at the appointed hour and greeted his friend with a huge grin and a slap on the back.

"Come on in," he bellowed, not realising that his voice was portraying his excitement by going up a few octaves, "Grace is just seeing to the guests' dinner first, which gives us time for a beer."

"Grand," said Elliot, following Dick into the private sitting room, "Sounds smashing."

The men sat chatting for half an hour over cold beer and peanuts. They could hear Grace clattering around in the kitchen as she ferried plates to and from the guest dining room, the smells of fresh plaice, and then jam roly poly pudding wafting around in the air.

"We'll be eating in the kitchen, as usual," Dick commented, "But Grace has done the table up all fancy with a white cloth and flowers."

"She shouldn't have gone to any trouble on my account," Elliot Moss grumbled, "I'm just happy to be here."

"Oh, you know Grace," chuckled Dick, "She loves making a fuss over the dinner table."

It wasn't long afterwards that Grace popped her head around the living room door and announced that dinner was ready. She greeted their guest with a huge smile and a peck on the cheek.

"Elliot, I'm so glad you could come," she cooed, not quite knowing what else to say.

Elliot Moss nodded and thanked her sincerely for the invitation.

As the two men seated themselves at the round kitchen table, Grace plated up the meals and opened another two bottles of beer. The food looked delicious and she served it up proudly.

"Goodness me Grace, that looks delicious," Elliot remarked, feasting his eyes on the fish in parsley sauce, new potatoes and pile of vegetables on his plate, "Are you trying to feed me up?"

Grace tutted and fluttered her eyes, "Just eat up and enjoy it."

The conversation over dinner was a little stilted at first, with Grace and Dick not quite knowing whether to mention Betty or not, but after a while Elliot made several references to her which eased his hosts' minds. The last thing they had wanted to do was upset the widower, who had obviously taken his wife's death very hard. Poor Elliot, Grace thought, he was devoted to his elegant and charming better half.

"That was the best meal I've had in ages," Elliot Moss announced as he put the last morsel of fish into his mouth, "I'm fit to burst now. Thank you Grace."

"Oh don't be silly," Grace replied, her cheeks turning pink, "That lovely fresh fish is courtesy of Robbie Powell the fishmonger. He catches it himself you know."

Elliot nodded, "Still, you've cooked it to perfection Grace, and the sauce was grand."

Dick coughed and nudged his friend cheekily, "Aye, Robbie Powell spends more time here than he does at home you know." He winked at Grace to let her know it was a harmless joke.

"Is that a fact?" laughed Elliot, "I hope you get a discount on your fish then!"

Grace turned red and started clearing plates from the table. It was none of anyone's business that she and Robbie had shared interests, she thought indignantly, not even Dick's.

She silently served pudding while the men continued to talk, and then poured herself a glass of wine.

"So, how are you coping Elliot?" she asked, trying to add an edge of sympathy to her tone, "Is there anything that you need help with?"

"It's been eight years Grace," Elliot answered, "I've kind of got used to doing things for myself now."

Both Dick and Grace were taken aback, had it really been that long since Betty Moss had died?

"Yes, of course," Grace said softly, putting a hand on the man's arm, "I just meant, we're here for you now, just like in the old days."

Elliot nodded and pushed his chair back from the table. "I guess I could use a hand sorting out Betty's things," he admitted, "You know, her magazines and stuff, the house is a bit cluttered."

"Of course," Grace sighed, "Dick and I can both help you with that."

"We could have a rummage sale," Dick cut in, "You know, make a bit of money for you."

Grace kicked him hard under the table and glowered, "Maybe that's not such a good idea Dick."

But Elliot was smiling now, "That's a great idea," he agreed, "The money could go to a good cause, like the children's home in Gallow Rock, Betty would love that."

Grace sighed, poor man, he's still thinking of his wife in the present tense.

A few days later, with Grace busily cleaning the guest house and preparing her meal plan for the week, Dick found himself at a loose end and decided to wander down to the beach to see when Elliot was ready to start clearing the house of his dead wife's belongings. It wasn't a job that he relished but it was something that he could actually do properly and he knew that his help would be appreciated.

"Morning," Dick called as he approached the wooden post to which Elliot tied the donkeys during the day,

Elliot popped his head up from checking Pandora's hooves and smiled as his friend approached.

"Alright Dick," he grinned, "What brings you down here? Is the betting shop closed?"

Dick feigned a sulk and folded his arms, "I'll have you know I've already put my bets on for today."

Elliot laughed and rolled his eyes, "Thought as much, you're a devil Dick Thomas."

Dick quickly explained the real reason for his visit and waited for his friend's response.

"Look, I'll be honest with you Dick," Elliot sighed, gently stroking the donkey's back, "I'm not sure I'm up to it. Do you think you could make a start without me? I can give you the key."

Dick was a bit flummoxed and didn't quite know what to say, "Well. Ok. But how will I know what to clear out? he asked, "There might be things you want to keep."

"All sorted," his friend beamed, "I've already put the things to be thrown out in the dining room, they're piled up on the table."

Dick was still unsure about going alone but he reluctantly took the key that Elliot was holding out to him.

"Alright," he agreed, "I'll take all the stuff up to my shed until Grace can sort out the sale. I'll have to go and fetch my wheelbarrow to carry it in."

"Ah, thanks Dick," Elliot beamed, "You don't know how much I appreciate this."

Dick waved his hand and turned to leave, "I'll bring the key back later," he called.

Elliot Moss stood watching the large man leave. Dick had put on more than a few pounds in the last few years he noted, must be all that good food that Grace was feeding him. Funny couple though, he thought silently, no children, no real hobbies and no holidays. It must be a hard life running the Sandybank day in and day out, he considered, no time for each other and very little time without someone or other needing their help. Maybe there's some way I can assist them, Elliot pondered, as a gesture of my appreciation.

Dick pushed the key into the lock of Elliot Moss's front door and stepped into the little terraced house. The air still held that strange musty smell and the first thing he decided to do was open some windows. He reckoned it had been a while since the sea breeze had entered Elliot's home and ridding it of the stale air would do it the world of good. He reached up and slid the latch off the sash window, sliding it slowly upwards until he could feel the gentle wind on his face. He then looked around the room, noting the dust free surfaces and carefully placed cushions. It was obvious that Elliot had no problem doing housework, but the décor really needed an update, everything looked so old and tired.

Dick left the sitting room and wandered down the hallway. He popped his head into the small kitchen, which was neat with nothing on the worktops. Only a single glass remained on the draining board. The pale blue cupboard doors were old and in desperate need of a new coat of paint but the stainless steel taps sparkled and the linoleum on the floor had obviously been scrubbed quite recently.

Turning right at the end of the hall, Dick opened the last door, which was next to the staircase, He presumed this was where he would find Elliot's 'clutter' and sure enough it was the dining room, tucked away at the back of the small house. The curtains were closed, with just the faintest hint of sunlight coming from a gap between the curtains. Dick padded over to window and drew the drapes back, squinting as the light flooded in. It was only then that he could see the items piled up on the oval mahogany table. There were lots of women's magazines, an old Singer sewing machine, balls of wool and knitting needles, several cookery books and a heap of novels, just the kind that Grace was always reading. There were a lot of miscellaneous kitchen goods that Dick had no idea what they were or what to do with them, but it didn't matter, there would be a woman somewhere who could convince herself that she couldn't live without this or that item. He sighed and grabbed the sewing machine. It was heavier than it looked, so perhaps he would need more trips with the wheelbarrow than first expected. This was going to be a very long day.

Grace watched from her vantage point at the kitchen window as her husband unloaded the heaps of fashion and hairstyle magazines, and thought back to her younger days when Betty Moss had been the envy of all the other women in the town. She'd had a way of adding little touches to her outfits that just gave them an edge, Grace remembered fondly, a snazzy belt here or an embroidered shirt there. When Betty's parents had died within six months of each other, the young woman had stayed up north for a couple of months, sorting out their affairs and selling the property. Rumour had it that Betty Moss was a very rich woman following her inheritance but she never showed it. Anything that had been bestowed on her by her family was secured away for a rainy day, no immediate extravagances and no foreign holidays. It was ironic that Betty had met her future husband on the very beach on which he now still worked. Endless attempts had been made by her parents to split up the donkey ride owner and their only child, but love had won out and Betty had never regretted her choice. Grace wondered why the couple hadn't used some of their windfall to buy a better house or a motor car, but to all outsiders it seemed that their world had been enough just to be with each other.

As Dick wheeled his third load of jumble up the garden path, Grace appeared at the kitchen door with an ice-cold lemonade in her hand. Dick carefully set down the wheelbarrow and stretched.

"Here you go," Grace clucked, "That looks like thirsty work dear."

Dick took the offered glass and gulped it down in one go.

"Ah," he sighed, holding in a burp, "I needed that. Elliot's got more junk than he let on you know."

Grace eyed him quizzically, "What did you expect?" she asked, "We women like to collect things."

Dick grunted and trundled his load down to the shed. Grace watched and stopped him on his return.

"Were there any clothes?" she asked hopefully, "Betty was such a chic lady, she had lots of dresses."

Dick shrugged, "I didn't see any love. In fact, there weren't any clothes in there at all."

Grace was clearly disappointed. "Never mind," she sighed, "Maybe Elliot hasn't sorted them out yet."

Dick managed two more loads before a prolonged twinge in his lower back persuaded him to stop for the day. After filling the shed with the last of the magazines he walked slowly back down the hill to return Elliot's key. As he neared the beach, Dick could see that two of the donkeys had children seated in their saddles, ready to walk the length of the shore and a group of proud parents stood taking photos with their box brownie cameras. Dick decided to sit down on the wall and wait until Elliot had walked the mules back and forth before going over to him. He ached from head to toe and a few minutes rest was much needed. I wouldn't mind trying one of those ice-creams with a flake in it either, Dick thought, now scrabbling to his feet and going over to the vendor. Just the one though, he told himself, Well, perhaps one double cone!

A short while later, Elliot Moss had returned with the donkeys, and Dick was finished with his afternoon treat. The children chattered excitedly as they ran back to their waiting parents and Elliot stood watching with his hands on his hips. He loved his job, it was just a pity that it was only for a few months of the year. That was something that Betty had often chided him for, insisting that he find work on the farm when the summer season was over. She was right of course, Elliot admitted, they would never have survived otherwise. There had been too many occasions when Betty had needed new clothes or something for the house and he, as her husband, had been unable to provide. Luckily Betty's parents were well off and regularly sent her cheques or postal orders to spend on what she needed. It was strange that they only ever visited on Betty's birthday and at Christmas, Elliot remembered, but he guessed that might have been more to do with the distance between their homes than her family disapproving of Betty's choice of husband. He could see the look on Betty's mother's face right now, looking down her nose at him.

"I've done as much as I can for today."

Elliot Moss turned from his day-dreaming to see Dick holding out a key to him.

"Thanks ever so much," he said, "Did you manage to move much?"

"Oh aye, loads," Dick replied, puffing out his chest with pride, "Only a couple of barrow trips left."

"Well I'll do those," smiled Elliot, taking in Dick's weary face and slouching shoulders. "You've done more than enough and I thank you for it."

Dick said goodbye and turned to leave, stopping momentarily as he remembered Grace's question from earlier that afternoon.

"Were there any of Betty's clothes that you needed to clear out?" he asked casually.

"No, why would there be?" queried Elliot, clearly surprised by the question.

"Oh, no reason," called Dick as he walked away, "See you tomorrow."

A few evenings passed before Dick and Grace invited Elliot Moss to dine with them again. This time he had smartened himself up considerably and presented his hosts with a bottle of Spanish wine.

"Oh, I say," commented Grace, as she tried to read the label, "From Seville."

"Well, if truth be told, it was a holiday gift from a neighbour," Elliot confessed, "But I'll never drink it."

Grace gave a slight wrinkle of the nose and looked up at her guest, "Well, it will certainly be appreciated here," she said, "Now sit down, dinner won't be long."

As they tucked in to chicken and leek pie, Grace could feel Elliot's eyes upon her. She smiled nervously back at him and waited for him to say something. Dick was too busy eating to notice anything.

"Grace, I've been thinking," Elliot began, "Actually it came to my mind the other day when Dick asked me about Betty's clothes."

Grace scowled cross the table at her husband, tact had never been his strong point. Instead of speaking she focused on Elliot who was obviously eager to continue.

"Well, I gave it some thought and I realised that Betty has a couple of dresses just hanging there in the wardrobe, it's a pity for them to go to waste."

Grace smiled politely, feeling a bit strange about the topic of conversation and sipped her wine slowly.

"If there's anything that you might like, you know, party frocks and suchlike, I'm sure Betty would want you to have them," Elliot Moss concluded, looking glad that he'd finally got the words out.

Grace nodded and blinked quickly, "Thank you Elliot, I know that Betty had some beautiful dresses, shall I pop round and have a look one day this week?"

"Yes, why not," the man answered slowly, "I'm sure it would be alright."

Grace looked confused for a second but let it pass, Elliot Moss was a funny man sometimes, but she knew that his heart was in the right place.

At the weekend, Grace found herself with no Saturday night meals to cook. There was a buffet at a local restaurant in town, with a band playing on the small stage, and all of the guests had decided to eat out. With Dick on his usual outing to the Miner's Arms, Grace decided to take the opportunity to have a look at Betty Moss's frocks. It was still early evening, and would be light for a good few hours, so she grabbed a lightweight cardigan and hurried off down the hill. As she stood knocking on the door, Grace wondered whether she should have made a prior arrangement first. It wasn't long before Elliot opened the door however and therefore too late to walk away.

"Good evening Grace," beamed Elliot Moss, "How lovely to see you. Have you come to see the dresses?"

"Yes, if that's alright with you," Grace stuttered, "I'm sorry just to come round unexpectedly."

"Don't be daft," the man assured her, as he opened the door wide enough for Grace to step inside, "It's always nice to have company, I don't get many guests these days."

"Thank you Elliot," Grace sighed as she took in the shabby surroundings for the first time, "You haven't changed much since Betty died then."

Elliot shook his head, "Change? Oh no, Betty wouldn't approve of me changing things."

Grace smiled politely, acknowledging once again that this poor man was still mourning the death of his wife. She silently wondered how long it would take for him to accept that she was gone.

"Would you like a drink?" Elliot offered, making a move towards the kitchen, "I've got coffee or beer, and there might even be some lemon barley in the fridge."

Grace shook her head, "No thank you, I can't stop long."

Elliot Moss took the hint and realised that Grace just wanted to see Betty's outfits and then get home.

"I'm guessing that you and Betty were about the same size," he commented, putting his foot on the bottom step of the staircase, "Come on up, there's too many dresses to bring down here."

Grace followed the house owner and wrinkled her nose at the musty smell coming from upstairs, she wondered whether the house was infested with mice, as it smelt slightly of droppings and moth balls, what a strange combination. Grace had a very keen sense of smell and was sure that she had never come upon such a strange combination of odours in her life before. She clutched her handbag tightly to her chest as she climbed the stairs and wished that she'd waited for Dick to come too.

"Here we are," announced Elliot Moss, standing with his hand upon a plain brown door, "We'll have to be quiet though."

Grace didn't understand, were the neighbours prone to listening in or something she wondered.

"Okay," she whispered, "Not another peep from me."

Elliot grinned and opened the door, "After you Grace," he said, allowing her to walk ahead.

Grace stepped into the bedroom and grimaced. It smelled even worse up here and it was quite hard to get her bearings, as the room had been plunged into semi-darkness by the drawn curtains.

"Elliot, I'm not sure that I feel comfortable up here," she began, turning toward the doorway once again, "Maybe this was a bad idea."

"Nonsense," the man insisted, going over to pull the curtains back along the rail, "She'll be over the moon to see you."

"Who....?" Grace faltered, trying to adjust her eyes to the light.

"Why Betty of course," Elliot announced, proudly motioning to a rocking chair in the corner, "She's been up here all alone waiting for you to come."

Grace felt the hairs start to rise on the back of her neck as she slowly turned around. Her palms had become sweaty and her joints were strangely stiff. Bravely she looked towards the corner.

There, sitting up straight in her wicker chair were the skeletal remains of Betty Moss, dressed in a pink frilly gown, with carpet slippers on her feet and a shawl around her shoulders.

Grace gasped as she tried to back away from the hideous sight, she moved her lips but nothing came out.

"It's alright, no need to be alarmed, Elliot soothed, "She'd rather be here than in some dark, damp grave."

Grace suddenly found her feet again and ran. In fact she didn't stop running until she had reached the safe walls of the Sandybank guest house and had all the doors double locked.

Chapter Ten

Sheila Collins

After her recent shock, Grace had refused to leave the house for a whole week. She had even missed her regular hair appointment and now her locks were starting to look frizzy and untamed. And so, putting on a brave face, and a lot of lipstick, Grace prepared herself for a trip to Maureen's salon. Dick had persuaded her not to report Elliot to the authorities but it had become quite a bone of contention between the two of them.

"Right, I'll be off then," Grace barked at her husband as he tramped in from getting his morning paper, "Now don't forget, if I'm not back, Mr. Lewis will be here around lunchtime, so you'll need to be around to check him in. He's staying in the yellow room."

"No problem," Dick grunted, sitting himself down. He then suddenly looked up at Grace and added, "There's a car up by the Meacham's again, with two men in it. They were there yesterday as well."

"So why don't you go and ask them what they want?" his wife snapped.

Dick wiped his nose with a huge white handkerchief and shook his head, "They're probably just admiring the view, or a couple of love-birds looking for peace and quiet."

"Humph, you're an idiot Dick Thomas," Grace shouted as she slammed the back door.

However, as Grace opened the front gate, she could clearly see the car that Dick had referred to parked further up the cliff road, just past the Meacham's house. It looked slightly familiar, but she couldn't think for the life of her who it belonged to. So, not worrying too much, she hurried off down the hill to get her hair revamped.

Meanwhile Dick had gone upstairs to open the window in the yellow bedroom, he wanted to show Grace that he was mindful of their guests and that this was a dual partnership not just her venture. He still felt guilty for not allowing his wife to call the police about Elliot Moss, but he just couldn't bear the thought of his good friend ending up in prison or a lunatic asylum, besides, what harm was he doing? He didn't like the authorities much anyway, and the further away they were, the happier he was.

At five to twelve the doorbell rang and a very thin and wizened man with round spectacles stood on the step. Dick could see his outline through the rippled glass of the front door and laughed. Not another single old bloke looking for fun at the seaside, he thought.

"Hello there," he greeted the gentleman, stepping aside to allow the man to enter, "Mr. Lewis I presume? If I could just get you to sign the guest book, then I'll show you up to your room."

The man smiled, showing a large gap in his front teeth, "I say Mr. Thomas, how lovely to meet you. It's a fabulous day isn't it? I needn't have put my blazer on this morning."

Dick stood waiting for the guest to fill in his details. As he looked at the man from behind, he could clearly see that Mr. Lewis was going bald on the centre of his crown and he stooped with a slight hunch in his shoulders. He must be at least sixty, Dick thought, and he hasn't worn well at all.

"There we are," sighed Mr. Lewis straightening up and putting the pen down, "I must say I'm rather looking forward to getting some sea air and sampling Mrs. Thomas's meals."

"Aye, she's a grand cook," Dick admitted, "Now then, let me carry your case and show you to your room."

Grace hadn't had to explain to Maureen O'Sullivan why she'd cancelled her appointment the week before, as the salon was busy that particular Thursday and Maureen flitted between clients while her new assistant shampooed, swept and made cups of tea. In fact, it was so busy that Mrs. Cole had managed to stay awake due to all the activity around her.

"See you next week," Maureen told Grace as she took payment from her, "We'll have a proper catch up then. Oh, and did I tell you that Sheila Collins is back in town?"

"Really?" Grace asked raising an eyebrow, "Now there's a name from the past."

"Moved back here for a quieter life apparently," Maureen continued, "What a turn up for the books."

Grace stood thinking for a few seconds but didn't answer. Instead she took her change, left a few shillings in the tip jar and wandered outside. Sheila Collins, she mused, well what a surprise!

Now it has to be said that Grace had actually given Sheila Collins a lot of thought over the years. After all, they were best friends in senior school and had spent every spare moment together, writing poems, spying on boys that they fancied and listening to the latest hits on the radio. It was hardly credible that Sheila had returned, after all everyone thought she had settled for good when she moved away with her husband, Terry. They made a lovely couple, and Terry was so hard-working, doing long hours as a self-employed plumber. The news of their move back to the beach was enough to put a spring in Grace's step as she turned towards home. But then she stopped, suddenly aware of a pair of eyes watching her. She slowly turned towards the sandy shore and saw Elliott Moss looking at her. He nervously raised his hand and smiled. Grace felt the hairs begin to prickle up on her neck and quickly walked on. She felt delighted with her new perfectly styled hair-do and it had given a much needed boost to her spirits, so Elliott Moss was not going to cause Grace's lifted mood to be ruined.

"Is everything alright Dick?" Grace asked as she put down her handbag and reached for the kettle, "Has Mr. Lewis arrived yet?"

"Oh yes," Dick nodded, "Another single old gent, he checked in about half an hour ago."

"Oh, well, I expect he's come down here to get some sea air and a bit of peace and quiet," Grace sighed, "We should be grateful that the single room is getting plenty of use this summer."

Dick took his jacket off the hook and looked closely at his wife, "I'm just popping out for a while. Your hair looks lovely by the way."

Grace flapped her hand and grunted, "Oh go on with you. Oh, and before I forget, Maureen just told me that Sheila & Terry Collins have moved back here, isn't that wonderful?"

Dick spun around sharply and coughed, "Oh, er, really? Well I never!"

Grace had already turned around to make herself a drink and missed the very disturbed look on her husband's face.

At dinner that night, Mr. Lewis was the first guest to enter the dining room. He was dressed in a smart tweed suit and sported a mustard coloured dicky bow with matching handkerchief, which was folded neatly in his breast pocket. As he entered, Grace looked up from setting out the condiments.

"Hello, you must be Mr. Lewis," she said, "I'm Grace Thomas, sorry I missed you this morning."

The gentleman eyed her approvingly and inclined his head, "Not to worry, I was well looked after by your capable husband. I must say, you have a beautiful home Mrs. Thomas."

Grace beamed with delight, she loved it when her guests appreciated the comfortable surroundings.

"Now then, you take a seat and I'll have dinner on the table in just a few minutes," she gushed, pulling out a chair for the elderly man, "I've made liver and onions tonight, or there's pork chops if you prefer."

Mr. Lewis sat down and took in the neat table setting and carefully folded napkins, "Liver and onions sounds wonderful thank you."

Grace returned to the kitchen to fill a pitcher of water for her guest and reflected upon her first impression of Mr. Lewis. He certainly looked as though he was worth a bob or two, she thought.

The following day, as Grace was taking a batch of apple pies out of the oven, Robbie Powell arrived with the fish. He didn't stay for his usual cup of tea and slice of cake, explaining to Grace that he had extra deliveries to make this week. It looked as though business was really picking up.

"Well, at least take one of these home with you," Grace insisted, already wrapping a clean cotton cloth tightly around one of the apple pies, "And make sure you pop in to see me during the week, I've got an idea for one of your romance stories."

"I will," Robbie grinned, brushing his thick curls out of his eyes, "I'll look forward to hearing about it."

"Oh, Robbie?" Grace called, just as the fisherman was heading out through the back door, "Do you happen to know where the Collins family are living?"

Robbie turned back and shifted his delivery basket to rest it on his hip, "They're in the old crofter's cottage down Montgomery Lane. Want me to drop in a message?"

"No thanks," Grace answered wistfully, "I think I'll pop down there myself, and maybe take them a welcome home gift."

"Right you are," Robbie replied, grabbing the door handle, "See you later Grace."

That afternoon, with an apple pie wrapped up neatly in a gingham cloth and tied with a red ribbon, Grace left instructions with Dick on what to set out for afternoon tea, should any of the guests require it, She strolled down the cliff road, oblivious to the dark car that now kept its daily vigil near the Meacham's house, and headed left past the school, glancing momentarily at Hilda Price's house, and carried on towards Montgomery Lane. The road didn't lead anywhere, but trailed off into a track that served both the local farm and a moderately steep hill with an old abbey at the top.

The old crofter's cottage was a white-washed stone building half-way down the lane, and it had obviously received some recent care and attention. There were new wooden window boxes full of pansies, a brightly painted red front door and brand new floral drapes hanging at the two front windows. Grace rapped gently on the door and waited. A few seconds later it was opened wide by a woman of similar age, stature and build to Grace. She recognised Sheila Collins immediately.

"Oh my goodness!" Grace squealed, "You really did come back!"

Sheila Collins blinked and gave a faint smile, "Grace, how lovely, erm, come in."

Sheila Collins led the way down a cool passageway to the kitchen at the rear of the cottage, where two teenage children sat chatting and eating jam sandwiches at the table. They both looked up as their mother entered.

"Lucy, Martin," she explained, "This is my old school friend Grace."

"Hello," they both chimed, automatically shuffling their chairs around for Grace to sit down.

"Hello dears," Grace replied, "Lovely to meet you. Last time I saw you, you were both just toddlers."

The young girl looked curiously at her mother's friend, "Sorry, I don't remember you."

"Oh, never mind," cooed Grace, "It must be over ten years ago. Anyway, Sheila I've brought you a little house-warming gift." She set the pie down on the table and looked at her friend admiringly.

"You look wonderful," she gushed, "The years have been very kind to you."

"You too," smiled Sheila Collins, "It's a pity Terry's not here, he would have loved to see you again."

"Nonsense," Grace tutted, "There will be plenty of time for catching up now that you're back."

"Yes, of course," Sheila sighed, "But I've still got a lot to do to the cottage, so I'll be busy for a while."

She wasn't sure, but Grace thought she sensed a slight frostiness in her friend's demeanour. It was slightly puzzling as the two women had parted as the best of friends when Sheila and her husband moved away. Grace had written to Sheila for a while too, but the replies had always been short notes, usually explaining that her friend was too busy to visit or tired from taking care of her two young offspring. Of course, Grace understood how married life had a way of making the years fly past, and with only eighteen months between her babies, Sheila must have had a hectic life in those first few years. Grace reflected upon how the birthday and Christmas cards had eventually stopped. Had she said or done something to upset her friend without even realising?

"Will you stay for a cup of tea," Sheila offered.

"Not today," Grace replied, "I've got lots of guests who'll be waiting for their afternoon treats."

Despite actually being free from ties for the next hour, Grace had forced herself to decline refreshments, feeling that the other woman's gesture had been half-hearted and obligatory. She turned to leave.

"Well, it was good of you to call," Sheila smiled, "And thank you for the apple pie."

Grace stepped back out into the sunlight and twirled around to look at her old school chum.

"Well, it's lovely to see you again," she said sadly, wishing that their first meeting after all these years had been more joyful, "Perhaps you and Terry would like to pop round for a drink one evening."

"Perhaps," Sheila repeated, not sounding very convincing, "Goodbye Grace, see you soon."

It wasn't until later that evening, with dinner plates cleared and guests retired to either the sitting room or out and about doing various activities that Grace had a chance to sit down and reflect upon the events of the day. She had been so looking forward to catching up with her long lost friend, hoping to both rekindle their former closeness and catch up with all the events of Sheila's life since moving away, but none of that had happened. Grace had no idea why Sheila should be so, what was it? Cold, uncaring, indifferent, towards her. She couldn't for the life of her think what might have happened to cause it.

"Dick," she started, glancing across at where her husband stood fiddling with the knob on the portable radio, "I went to see Sheila Collins today."

"Did you now," he muttered, sticking his tongue out as he searched the channels, "And?"

"Well, she wasn't exactly friendly," Grace admitted, folding her arms tightly across her chest, "It was quite sad really, we were so close in our younger days."

"Well, people change," Dick grunted, "Probably thinks she's too good for us now."

"They live in the crofter's cottage for goodness sake!" Grace reminded him, "It's not even detached."

Dick stopped what he was doing and sighed, "Look love, people change, that's all I'm saying."

Grace snatched up her romance novel and pretended to read. Not me, she thought, not me.

Next morning Mr. Lewis was once again the first guest to show his face in the dining room. Dressed for a day out walking in his khaki shorts and hiking boots, he looked every inch the explorer, with a little knapsack equipped with maps, compass, sun hat and fruit. He was looking much healthier too.

"I say Mrs. Thomas," he asked as Grace delivered a teapot to his table, "Would you mind making me up a flask of tea dear? I'm intending to walk up to those ancient ruins at Friar's Peak today."

"Of course, no problem at all," Grace replied, "I'll make you a packet of sandwiches to take too."

"Oh, that would be awfully kind," the old man smiled, "That would be simply marvellous."

"Not at all," the landlady assured him, "Nothing is too much trouble for guests at the Sandybank."

As she returned to the kitchen Grace chided herself. Why did she always say these things? Giving herself more work than was absolutely necessary and wasting time being polite to fuddy-duddy old men! If only I could be the one staying in a hotel for a week, she mused, having someone wait on me hand and foot, pandering to my every need. Thoughts of taking a holiday came rushing to the fore again, maybe she was just tired, or maybe she really did need a break after all. Grace reminded herself to check how much money was in their bank account, surely a little trip somewhere wasn't totally out of the question.

"I say, it was absolutely fantastic up there amongst those abbey ruins," Mr. Lewis puffed breathlessly as he came in through the front door that afternoon, "I could see for miles, got some great photos."

Grace was just coming down the stairs and she stopped abruptly, taking in the man's windswept hair and dusty walking boots. Mr. Lewis followed her gaze down to his feet and shrugged.

"I'd better take these off hadn't I?" he asked, "They're just a tad too dirty."

"If you don't mind," Grace sniffed, trying to inconspicuously check for traces of mud on her hall carpet, "I'll fetch an old newspaper for you to put them on."

"I say, I saw Mr. Thomas on my way back," the visitor continued, "Although I didn't stop to chat as he seemed rather engrossed in conversation with a lady."

Grace pricked her ears up. "Oh, where was that?" she asked casually, pretending not to care.

"Just outside a lovely white cottage," Mr. Lewis remarked, "Along the lane that leads to the nature trail, towards the ruins."

He didn't need to continue, Grace knew exactly where he was describing, and she knew exactly which lady it was that Dick would have been talking to. He's probably been down to see Sheila to find out what's wrong, she pondered, hoping that all could be explained and they could begin their friendship anew. How considerate of Dick, she thought, unless, of course, he'd been down there looking for Terry Collins. Yes, that was more likely, Dick would be in search of help with the plumbing, she concluded.

As they tucked in to a ham and egg salad that evening, Grace waited patiently for Dick to tell her about his conversation with Sheila Collins. When, after a twenty minute silence, no details had been forthcoming, Grace ventured into the murky waters of trying to extract the truth.

"Did you see anybody particular on your travels this afternoon?" she enquired casually.

"No," Dick replied, "Well, except I did bump into Oscar, and I said a quick hello to Robbie's dad."

"Oh," Grace quipped, raising her eyebrows, "Nobody else?"

Dick thought for a moment, scratching his head, "No, I don't think so love."

"You didn't happen to see Terry Collins?" she pushed, "Or Sheila?"

Dick visibly stiffened but continued trying to stab a rolling pickled onion on his plate, "No, why would I want to see Terry Collins?"

"No reason, just wondered," Grace lied.

She watched her husband as he succeeded in stabbing the pickle. Either he was hiding the truth very well or Mr. Lewis had been mistaken in his observations. She assumed it was the latter but just to be doubly sure, she would question their guest again the following day.

Over a plate of scrambled eggs, mushrooms and toast the next morning, the elderly guest relayed what he had seen to Grace, assuring her that he would know her husband anywhere, even a police line-up!

"I do hope I haven't caused any bother by mentioning it," the old man fussed, "I was simply making conversation you see. But yes, it was Mr. Thomas, most definitely. I never forget a face."

"Oh, it's nothing," Grace fibbed, "He lost something, so I was just wondering where he'd been, so that we could retrace his steps."

"Oh, well perhaps I could help?' Mr. Lewis offered kindly, setting down his knife and fork.

"No, it's fine," Grace snapped, off-handedly, "There's really no need."

Mr. Lewis peered over his round spectacles and watched as the heat rose in his landlady's face. Either she was lying, he figured, or Mr. Thomas has been a naughty boy.

A few uneventful days passed, with Dick going about his daily routine and Grace busy catering for her guests varied needs. A young family had arrived & now occupied the two connecting rooms at the back of the house, which gave Grace no end of inspiration and she spent her afternoons making lemonade iced lollies and chocolate cakes for the children. Mr. Lewis disappeared after breakfast each morning, either for a ramble or bird-watching trip and returned dead on four o'clock each afternoon in anticipation of a pot of tea and a selection of the proprietor's homemade delicacies. All in all, Grace was kept busy but nothing so strenuous that she felt need to complain.

Therefore, with being kept on her toes and not venturing beyond her own four walls, it wasn't until Thursday morning that Grace heard the mention of her former best friend's name again.

"I see that Sheila's settled back in," Maureen O'Sullivan commented as she looped Grace's hair around plastic rollers, "She's always down on the front sitting on the harbour wall."

"Really?" Grace quipped, raising an eyebrow in surprise, "I thought she'd be busy decorating."

"Well, obviously not," the hairdresser replied casually, "Your other half always stops to chat with her."

"Oh, erm, yes I know," Grace lied, feeling hurt that Dick hadn't once mentioned seeing Sheila Collins.

Maureen gave her client a confused look in the mirror. Which was it she wondered, did Grace know about Maureen hanging around talking to her husband or not?

"I suppose you'll have seen a lot of her," she pushed, "What with you and Sheila being best friends."

"Oh, really, that was a very long time ago," Grace huffed offhandedly, "Now, am I ready for the drier?"

Arriving back at the guest house later than usual, after spending an hour browsing the bookshop and buying flowers in the market, Grace was once again eaten up by her thoughts. Why hadn't Dick felt the need to tell her he'd seen Sheila Collins? Were they meeting secretly, she wondered, or perhaps not so secretly if they had arranged a rendezvous in front of the whole town!

"Alright love," Dick asked, entering the kitchen with a trug full of herbs from the garden, "It's a grand day, the sun's cracking the flag-stone's out there. I thought you might need these for cooking."

Grace spun around to face her husband, there were no tell-tale signs of guilt on his face and it looked by all intents and purposes that he'd been here in the garden all morning. But then it hit her. Of course he would be here, as Grace had been into town and her two-timing husband couldn't risk being seen.

"Thank you," she replied cautiously, "Are you going out this afternoon?"

"Don't be daft, I always go out for a walk in the afternoons don't I?" Dick snorted, "Unless you need me to stay here?"

"No," Grace snapped sharply, "I just wondered."

"Look love," Dick soothed, trying to snuff out the initial sparks of a full-scale argument before it started, "I don't know what you're getting at, but I've been really busy this morning. I was up at the crack of dawn finishing the patio."

"What?" Grace squealed, "It's finished?"

"Yes, love," Dick beamed widely, "I put the last slabs down about an hour ago."

Grace raced outside to take a look at her husband's handiwork. Sure enough, the paving slabs were grouted and swept, creating a wide enough area to place a table and chairs in the sunshine.

"Oh Dick," she cried, "How wonderful."

As the pair stood admiring their new patio, Grace suddenly noticed that there was washing on the line.

"Mr. Lewis had to check out a day early," Dick explained, following his wife's gaze, " Don't worry love, his money is all present and correct in the tin."

"Oh, I see," Grace muttered, "Well thanks for putting the sheets in the wash."

"We'll need to leave those slabs to set properly for a few days," Dick explained, turning to go back inside, "Then we can see about getting a nice table and chairs."

Grace had momentarily forgotten about her husband's supposed liaison with Sheila Collins but seeing him walking away reminded her to be vigilant once again.

"Where did you say you were going?" she enquired.

"Nowhere in particular," Dick called, as he sat on the back step changing his gardening shoes for a pair of lace-up leather boots, "Just for a walk."

"Oh, I see," Grace murmured, "See you later then."

For the umpteenth time that day, it occurred to Grace that she should follow Dick to see if her fears bore any rationality. At the very least, she could be proved wrong and nobody need be any the wiser. So, rushing upstairs to change into a pair of flat shoes, old trousers, a white jumper, dark sunglasses and a plain headscarf, Grace was out through the door five minutes after her husband. She could still see him lumbering down the cliff road towards the harbour and knew that if she walked quickly, she could keep at a safe enough distance to keep him in her sights but remain unobserved. It wasn't long before he stopped to talk to someone at the harbour wall.

Grace sucked in her breath as she watched Sheila Collins grasp Dick firmly by the arm and flutter her eyelashes provocatively at him. Dressed in a tight fitting red polyester dress, Grace's former school friend had unbuttoned her clothing just enough to reveal a hint of her cleavage, she wore far too much make-up for a warm sunny day too. As the scene unfolded, Sheila tossed her hair back over her shoulder. Dick was saying something but Grace was too far away to hear. She stepped behind a tall red post box and peeped out to see if there were any intimate gestures. For a few seconds, Sheila seemed to be pleading with Dick but he certainly didn't look very impressed and started to walk away.

"What if I tell her?" Grace could hear Sheila calling, "What would you do then?"

Dick swung around and flapped his hands clumsily. Typical Dick, Grace thought, as she watched him.

"Shhhh woman," he remonstrated, moving closer, "Keep your voice down."

From her vantage point, Grace could see her husband steering Sheila Collins by the elbow. He pulled her down the ramp to the beach and gestured for her to sit on one of the many deckchairs set out there. The seaside was full of tourists, but nobody took any notice of the middle-aged pair sitting side by side, except for Grace, who had scuttled along the front as quickly as she could and was now crouched behind the harbour wall, right above where Dick and her former school friend were talking in hushed tones.

"If you tell Grace anything," Dick was saying sternly, "Well, I'll not be responsible for my actions."

"Are you threatening me Dick Thomas?" Sheila Collins snapped.

"No," Dick whined, "I'm just saying there's no need for all this,"

"Oh, come off it," the woman continued, "We had a great time, you and me, and now I'm back"

Grace put her hand over her mouth to stifle a cry, she couldn't believe what she was hearing.

"Sheila love," Dick was saying, trying to soothe the woman, "It was a very long time ago."

"Mmmm, and on the night before your wedding too," she teased.

Grace had heard quite enough, and fully intended to run home, but her legs had turned to jelly.

"Look, I'm happy with Grace," she could hear her husband saying, "Just leave it Sheila."

"Well what if I told her about our little affair," Sheila Collins threatened, her voice shrill and shaky, "Do you think she would ever forgive you?"

"So, what do you want?" Dick snapped, losing his temper, "Just tell me, is it money?"

Grace heard Sheila laugh, a sarcastic tone, clipped and nasal, "Money? Huh? Where would you ever get a decent sum of cash from? No, I want us to come to an arrangement, maybe meet up once or twice a week for a little, you know, fun."

"I've got money of my own stashed away," Dick told the woman indignantly, "Money that Grace doesn't know about."

"Oh, have you now," Sheila Collins teased, "Maybe you can satisfy my body and my pocket then!"

Grace couldn't take any more and crawled along the harbour wall until she could safely stand up without risk of being seen by the couple on the beach. Her breathing had become laboured in panic and more than a few people were staring at her, wondering what this woman in sunglasses had been doing on her hands and knees. Grace took a deep breath, brushed down her trousers and broke into a run. As she reached her garden gate she stopped for a moment to let her heartbeat settle. Grace was far too preoccupied with her thoughts to notice the two men sitting in the dark car outside the Meacham's house. They were watching her intently.

Sitting at the kitchen table, Grace placed both of her palms flat on the cool surface and told herself to calm down. She needed to think clearly and compose herself for when Dick returned. She realised that her first action must be to remove all semblance of her disguise and act as normally as possible. Grace's mother had prepared her fully for a disaster such as this and she would carry out the instructions to the letter. The first step was to ascertain all of the facts before making a rash decision, second step was to secure her finances from risk of loss should a separation ensue. It occurred to her that she also needed to find Dick's secret savings. Finally she would seek retribution.

Therefore, now dressed once again in her pale pink cotton dress and flowered apron, Grace took her baking ingredients from the pantry and began the process of making a cake. All is normal, she told herself. In the words of mother's motto, facts first, fury later.

A smile played upon her lips as Grace creamed together sugar and butter in a bowl. If she feigned ignorance and let matters play out by themselves without a hint that she knew of the dreadful betrayal by Dick and her so-called best friend, Grace knew that ultimately she would be able to turn the scenario to her own advantage. And that is what she fully intended to do.

Chapter Eleven

The Harrison Brothers

It was Friday, the day after Grace had discovered her husband's betrayal. Thankfully the guests had kept her busy enough to avoid con-
frontation with Dick but she could feel goosebumps on her arms every
time he entered or left the house. The hardest part was trying to carry
on as normal, pretending to enjoy cooking meals and cleaning but,
underneath, the gravity of what she knew was tearing Grace apart.
She hadn't slept a wink the night before and had lain awake listening
to Dick snoring, and at moments also wishing that she had the nerve
to drive a knife into his heart. Perhaps then, he would understand the
pain that he had caused. It didn't matter that twenty years had passed
since his night of infidelity, it mattered that he had been unfaithful to
her, it mattered that he was obviously thinking about doing it again
and it mattered even more that it was with Sheila Collins.

Biting her bottom lip to control the anger building within her, Grace
carefully wrote out receipts for the two families who were checking
out that morning. The Shuttleworth's were already packing their suitcases upstairs, whilst the Morgan family had taken one last walk on
the beach in search of shells for the children to take home. Neither
family had caused one iota of inconvenience, finishing their meals,
complimenting Grace on her beautiful home and quietly playing board
games in the sitting room each evening. Grace felt ashamed that she
had been unable to conjure up a smile for the children that morning

at breakfast and, even now, as they came skipping down the stairs she was still looking glum.

"We're going on the train Mrs. Thomas," Peter Shuttleworth told her, "I love trains."

"That's great," she managed to reply, "I wish I could come with you."

The six year old giggled, "You have to stay here, and take care of your hotel."

Grace ruffled his hair and sighed, "Yes dear, I do don't I?"

As she reached up to put the old biscuit tin back on the shelf, in which she had deposited the guest's payments, there was a knock on the door and Robbie Powell entered. Grace had completely forgotten about her fish delivery, in fact she was unaware of which day of the week it was at the moment, and she looked as startled a rabbit caught in headlights as he put down his basket and helped to steady the stool that she was standing on.

"Hey, what's up Grace?" Robbie asked, alarmed at seeing the dark circles and red rims around her eyes, "Has something happened?"

It took just that one question for the whole sordid story to come pouring out and, making coffee for them both while Grace tearfully explained, the young fisherman stood rooted to the spot in shock.

"What are you going to do?" he finally coaxed, "Aren't you going to confront him?"

Grace blew her nose and shook her head, "Not yet, I'm still deciding how to handle things."

"Ok," Robbie soothed, desperately searching for the right words, "Maybe in time things won't seem quite so bad. Perhaps you should listen to what Dick has to say."

It was as though a red hot poker had been thrust at her, and Grace turned to look at the young man, furious and seething, "Not quite so bad?" she mocked, "This isn't one of your stupid romance stories!"

Robbie Powell stepped back a pace and busied himself with taking a small parcel of fish out of the basket, "I'm sorry Grace," he murmured, "I don't know what else to say."

"Promise me you won't tell a soul," she pleaded, "I couldn't bear the shame."

"Shhh," Robbie soothed, putting an arm around her shoulder, "You know you can trust me."

That afternoon, around two o'clock, Grace was just putting vases of freesias into the guest bedrooms when she heard the doorbell ring. That must be the new guests arriving, she thought, hurrying to answer the door, two single rooms for a week, for the Harrison brothers. She glanced out of the window and saw a dark coloured Ford Anglia parked outside.

As Grace ascended the stairs, she could see that Dick had managed to get himself there first and he now stood holding the door wide open to allow the two men to enter. She hadn't heard him come home at lunchtime, as she'd been busy hoovering upstairs but was sure that he would have helped himself to the plate of sandwiches that she had automatically made. Funny how you just go into auto-pilot in a crisis, she mused, stepping down into the hallway, Dick hadn't noticed any change in her and that was a bonus.

The two men stood holding their suitcases as Grace welcomed them to the Sandybank. They were both tall, but one a couple of inches more so than the other, dressed in casual slacks and polo shirts, and one wore a panama hat. They were obviously ready for an enjoyable week at the seaside.

"If you would just sign the register," Dick prompted, "Then I'll take your cases up to your rooms."

"Great," the taller man smiled, showing pearly white teeth, "Mr. and Mrs. Thomas, right?"

Grace ushered the men into the sitting room with the promise of tea and biscuits, while Dick sorted out their luggage.

"Please, call me Alf," the shorter Mr. Harrison told Grace, "We're looking forward to our stay."

"And I'm Eric," the other brother offered, "Nice to meet you Mrs. Thomas."

Grace gave the men a fake smile and went straight to the kitchen to make them a drink. Her heart really wasn't in being hospitable today, but she'd do her very best, she always did.

Meanwhile, in the sitting room, the Harrison brothers were discreetly having a good look around.

Grace managed to avoid Dick again that afternoon, as having deposited the gentlemen's suitcases, he pecked his wife on the cheek and wandered down to the town to carry out his usual tasks. She used the time wisely, searching high and low for the secret savings that she'd heard her husband mention to Sheila Collins. At the time, Grace had presumed that the money must be from winnings on the horses, but now she wasn't so sure. Ever since Dick had taken up those Sunday morning cycle rides with Oscar, she'd noticed a more confident air about him, but Dick didn't really have the common sense to keep secrets. By the time Grace had prepared a dinner of fish pie with green vegetables for her guests, he was back and sat reading the newspaper at the kitchen table.

"You alright love?" Dick asked casually, "You've been very quiet since last night."

Grace could feel the tears being to brim and fought to hold them back. Not now, she told herself, wait.

"I'm fine," she muttered, "Just the start of a summer cold coming I think."

"Best take some honey and lemon tonight then," Dick suggested, "This place can't tick without you."

Grace sniffed, oh the irony in that comment.

She said no more and silently took the hot meals through to the dining room, both hands trembling slightly. When she returned, Grace set Dick's dinner on the table in front of him and then poured herself a glass of wine.

"Where's yours?" he immediately asked, "Are you not hungry love?"

"No, not really," Grace replied, looking him straight in the eye and trying to stay composed, "Maybe I'll have some cheese and crackers later."

"You need to eat," Dick returned, shoveling fish pie into his mouth, "This is really good."

Grace turned away and stood by the sink, feeling sick at the very sight of her husband.

When Dick returned from his regular trip to the Miner's Arms, that evening, Grace was already in bed. She hadn't expected him home before eleven and was still sitting upright against her pillows, making notes in her diary. On hearing a heavy tread in the hallway she snapped the little book shut.

"Are you feeling any better love?" Dick asked, bounding into the bedroom like a child on a pogo stick. Grace could smell the beer on him and wrinkled up her nose.

"Not really," she huffed, "Anyway, I was just about to go to sleep."

As she reached across to turn off the bedside table, Dick started unbuttoning his shirt.

"I saw those two brothers in town," he told Grace, ignoring the fact that she was pulling the covers around her head, "Having a fish and chip supper at Angelo's café they were."

Grace lowered the eiderdown a fraction and perked her ears up, "Which brothers?"

"The one's that checked in here this afternoon, the Harrisons," he went on.

Grace crinkled her brow, confused. What would they be doing eating in town? True enough they hadn't eaten the meal that she'd served them, both telling her they'd had a big lunch earlier in the day, but then why would they go and buy food elsewhere? Was it that they didn't like her cooking, she wondered.

The next morning, Grace was up early, not having slept very well for a second night. She sat in the kitchen drinking coffee, waiting for the first of her guests to come down for breakfast. As it happened the two brothers arrived within minutes of each other.

"Good morning," she smiled stiffly, "What can I get you? A Full English? Kippers? An omelette?"

Eric Harrison looked at his brother across the table and raised his eyebrows.

"Just toast for both of us please Mrs. Thomas," Alf requested, showing his perfect teeth again.

"Really?" Grace checked, "No eggs, baked beans or mushrooms to go with it?"

"Plain toast will be just fine," Eric interjected, "We're not very hungry this morning. Thanks."

Well, it must be that fish supper you ate in Angelo's café last night, Grace tutted to herself sarcastically, there's no pleasing some folks!

Later that day, as Grace flicked the duster around the sitting room, she heard the phone ringing in the hallway. However, as she reached the door, Dick had beaten her to it and was now listening intently.

"Aye, we're fine thanks," he bawled into the receiver, "I'll just go and get Grace."

Grace stood still, amazed that she'd never noticed Dick's telephone manner before. It was the behaviour of an ageing crone to think you had to shout when talking to someone far away down the line.

"Ah, there you are," he smiled, seeing Grace in the doorway, "Your mother's on the blower."

"Tell her I'm not here," Grace whispered, checking that the phone was turned away from her, so that the caller couldn't hear, "Tell her I've gone into town for something."

"But she's ringing to test out her new phone line," Dick explained, in a low tone, "She's excited."

"I don't care," Grace breathed, "I'm not here!"

Her husband dutifully returned to the telephone and started on some long-winded tale about Grace having popped out on an errand. In the meantime, his wife had rushed to the bathroom to be sick. Just the thought of speaking to her mother right now made Grace's stomach churn. She knew she wouldn't be able to keep up the farce when she heard her voice, so for the present Grace had to avoid her parents at all costs, just until she had decided what to do.

Dick didn't bother to follow Grace upstairs, neither did he enquire, on her finally coming back down, why she hadn't wanted to speak to her mother. His wife had these funny moods sometimes, he reminded himself, best keep to yourself for a while Dick, he decided.

That evening, as Grace served ham salad to her other guests, Grace noticed the very obvious absence of the Harrison brothers. With it being a Saturday night, she wondered if they might have gone to eat in town again, or perhaps they'd had another huge lunch in the afternoon. They certainly hadn't had the decency to tell their host that they intended to eat out, so she covered their plates and put them in the chiller. If the men returned hungry later that evening she would be happy to give them their meals, but not before giving them a piece of her mind on etiquette first.

As it was, the Harrisons did come back to the guest house at a decent hour but went straight up to their rooms without seeking sustenance. Grace heard them come in, but didn't move from her chair.

On Sunday morning, with all the guests making the most of the wonderful sunshine, the Sandybank guest house was unusually quiet. Grace, still in a sullen mood, equipped herself with cleaning essentials and went upstairs to give each room a quick going over. She only intended to sweep, open windows and empty waste paper bins, so only an hour of her time would be necessary. After that she planned to do some accounting to check how much had been squirrelled away in the past few years and, if there was time, she would go down to the potting shed to look for Dick's money.

On opening the door to Alf Harrison's guest room, Grace immediately noticed the smell of cooked meat. As she walked further into the room the odour got stronger until, on reaching the dressing-table, it had reached its most pungent. She stooped down and pulled out the little blue bin from underneath. On the very top of the litter was a foil pie case. Grace could feel her blood pressure rising. One very strict rule that she expected all guests to adhere to was no food in the bedrooms. And why, oh why, she asked herself, had Alf Harrison needed to bring a meat pie back here to eat when she had provided him with a perfectly good meal included in his board money? She carefully picked the pie case up between thumb and forefinger, and dropped it gently into her open bin liner. She didn't have either the inclination or the energy to confront her guest at the moment, so she would let this incident go, just this once.

"Evening Mrs. Thomas," a cheerful voice called from the hallway as Grace opened the kitchen door.

"Ah, Mr. Harrison," she greeted the guest, "Will you and your brother be dining here tonight?"

"Erm, no I think we might go out tonight," Eric Harrison replied, looking at his brother, who nodded.

"Oh, right you are," Grace huffed, "Up to you."

"Mrs. Thomas," Alf Harrison began, coughing softly, "How many single guests would you say you have staying here every year?"

"Well, I don't rightly know," Grace snapped tiredly, "What a very strange question."

"Oh, just curious," Alf's brother explained, "We're thinking about erm, opening a hotel."

"What, just for single guests?" Grace asked, feeling very confused.

"Yes, well single men," Eric smiled, "Older men in particular, so how many on average?"

'What on earth are you suggesting?" the landlady questioned sharply.

Alf Harrison nudged his brother and winked, "Come on Eric, let's go for a pint."

After dinner, Grace settled back onto the sofa with one of her new romance novels, although her mind was far from fixed upon the dreamy characters and ideal settings. Instead, much to her own annoyance, Grace was thinking about the Harrison brothers. Alf and Eric's strange behaviour had started the very moment that they had arrived. Grace ran her fingers through her curls and tried to fathom what was wrong.

For a start, neither man seemed to like Grace's cooking, although they had only managed to eat toast and biscuits on the premises so far, which hardly constituted a meal. She began to worry that perhaps one of the other guests had made negative comments about the food, leaving the Harrison pair preferring to fend for themselves. Grace had also noticed that the brothers were very curious about the furnishings too, on more than one occasion she had entered a room to find one or other of the men looking behind cushions or flicking through the magazine rack. She worried that they were professional con-men, like she'd heard about on the radio some months before, although they seemed far too polite to be villains. Grace stopped herself from over-thinking matters and sighed, would she really be able to tell an honest man from a rogue if suspicions warranted it?

"I've made you a cup of tea," Dick announced, interrupting his wife's train of thought, "Shall I fetch you some biscuits to go with it?"

"What?" Grace asked, taking the china cup and saucer from his chubby hands, "No, no biscuits."

Dick hovered next to the sofa, looking at his hands. He coughed gently and began the sentence that he had carefully prepared some minutes before as he had waited for the kettle to boil.

"Look, I know I'm not the most intelligent or best-looking husband in the world," he started, "But I do know when there's something wrong with my wife. Grace, you've hardly said two words to me lately."

A faint smile played on Grace's lips as she recalled her mother's words, knowledge is power.

"If I've done something wrong, I'd rather you told me straight out," Dick continued, hardly pausing for breath, "It hurts to think you can't talk to me anymore."

Grace closed her eyes for a couple of seconds as she carefully chose her words, "HAVE you done anything wrong Dick?"

"Well, not that I can think of," her husband began slowly, "Perhaps I didn't realise."

"Then let's say no more about it," Grace said in a clipped voice, "Shut the door on your way out."

By Monday, Grace had become far more level-headed and was beginning to form a plan of action in her mind. Her intention was to take a European holiday, alone. Her time would be spent thinking about the state of her marriage and Dick's terrible betrayal, which hopefully would result in the correct decision. Grace had been brought up with strict morals and also believed that a marriage was always worth fighting for, but now she wondered whether their whole twenty something years together had been a complete sham. There were questions that Grace would prefer not to know the answers to, but she also knew that if those subjects were left alone to fester, she would be better off on her own. Ever since she had heard the two of them talking at the harbour, Grace had been kept awake by visions of Dick and Sheila canoodling together. It upset her deeply that her best friend had slept with the younger, handsome, funny Dick, rather than the older, fatter, sillier one. But then she realised something for the first time. Grace herself might not feel very inclined to make love with Dick these days, but THAT other woman obviously did. The thought made bile rise up in her throat again.

Therefore, that morning, Grace was determined to ask her father to drive her to the next town where she could book a holiday without the prying eyes or gossiping tongues of the other seaside residents. She would act responsibly, booking it for October, at the end of the British holiday season, but still warm enough in the Mediterranean towns to benefit both her health and mind. She didn't worry about withdrawing funds from the bank, Dick would never check anyway as he always trusted his wife to take care of any monetary issues. The only thorn in her side was Grace's need to confront Dick before she left for her chosen destination. It wouldn't be easy, but he would have to suffer whatever decision she came to. After all, Grace was the one hard done by.

As she gathered up a lightweight jacket and slipped her bank book into her handbag, Grace took a quick look around to make sure that nothing needed to be done before she left. It would only take her a couple of hours to do what she needed, but as was her conscientious nature, Grace still needed things to be perfect and undisrupted by her absence. It was as she dithered by the door that the telephone rang.

"Mr. Lewis?" Grace repeated, "No, I'm sorry he left some days ago."

She listened intently as the unseen person continued speaking.

"Well, no, I'm sorry I can't see how I can help," she told the caller, "Good day to you."

As Grace replaced the receiver in its cradle, she looked up to where eyes were watching her over the bannister. It was Alf Harrison.

"Everything alright?" he enquired, "Has someone gone missing?"

"No." Grace lied, opening the door, "It was nothing, wrong number."

Sitting in the car beside her father, Grace was biting her bottom lip. She'd asked him to pick her up outside the bank and from there they were now heading to the next town. Grace Thomas's father was a man of few words but every few minutes he gave his daughter a concerned look.

"How long do you think you'll be?" he asked, trying to put a cheery tone in his voice, although underneath he was worried that Grace was about to do something totally out of character. Although what that deed was, he hadn't for the life of him got a clue.

"Only about an hour," she assured him, patting his arm, "You go and have a coffee and a cream cake."

"I can come with you if you like?" Mr. Thomas offered, slowing the car down as they reached a junction, "Unless you'd rather I didn't?"

"Don't be silly," Grace giggled, "It's just boring stuff at the tax office, that's all."

"So why isn't Dick coming with you?" her father questioned, glancing across at the passenger's seat, "He should take responsibility for the finances."

"Oh, you are silly," Grace clucked, "Dick is useless at accounts, besides it'll be quicker if I fill in the forms by myself."

Satisfied with her answer, Grace's father pulled into a side street and parked the car.

"I'll see you in an hour," Grace assured him, "Back here, okay?"

Mr. Thomas locked the car and watched his only daughter scuttling off around the corner towards the tax office. What he didn't see, was Grace doubling back a couple of minutes later and going in the opposite direction towards the travel agency. She hated lying to her parents, but Grace dearly hoped that once everything was out in the open, they would understand her need for diplomacy.

On the way home, her father was much more talkative, allowing Grace the luxury of not having to speak very much. Apparently he had bumped into an old friend in the café and now regaled his daughter with tales of boyish escapades from their younger days. Feigning interest by smiling and laughing at regular intervals, Grace was able to give the impression that she was listening intently. Inside however, she was feeling both thrilled and terrified. Her holiday was booked for the middle of October and only a natural disaster was going to keep Grace from catching that flight.

At lunchtime, Dick came in from the garden to make himself something to eat. As Grace had popped out to 'take care of some errands', he hadn't yet been into town to fetch his newspaper and looked around for something to read. Not seeing anything more stimulating than a paperback romance, Dick sauntered into the living room to retrieve the little orange and white book that he was becoming so fond of. However, expecting to find the room empty, being his and Grace's personal space, it was occupied by the Harrison brothers. Not only were they in the wrong room, but Eric Harrison suddenly jumped as Dick entered.

"Alright there?" Dick said calmly, eyeing both men up, "This here's mine and the wife's private sitting room, sorry if we didn't explain that clearly enough."

"Oh, I'm so sorry old chap," Alf Harrison apologised, striding across to stand between his sibling and the landlord, "We didn't know, did we Eric?"

Eric Harrison shook his head and sidled around his brother to the doorway, "Very sorry Mr. Thomas, we'll leave you in peace."

Dick nodded and watched the men leave, noticing a suspiciously familiar orange book cover sticking out of Eric Harrison's trouser pocket. He wasn't one for making a fuss, but Dick knew that what he had seen was 'All This and Bevin Too'. Immediately, checking down the side of his favourite armchair, Dick's fears were confirmed immediately, his precious book was gone. Wringing his hands, he wondered what to do,

When Grace returned an hour later, Dick was sitting at the kitchen table with an empty plate in front of him, having just finished the remainder of an egg and cress sandwich.

"Did you get all your errands done?" he asked expectantly, getting up to wash his crockery.

"Yes thank you," Grace replied, her voice betraying just a hint of the excitement that she felt at having now executed the first part of her plan.

"Those Harrison fellows have stolen my book!" Dick blurted out unintentionally.

"What book?" Grace quizzed, setting her bag down carefully on a chair, "Oh, THE book?"

"Yes," Dick blushed, knowing full well what his wife thought about his reading material.

"Well, never mind," she said flippantly, taking her apron from the hook, "You can buy another."

"But Grace," Dick whined, taking her by the arm, "I have to have THAT one."

Ten minutes later, the guest house owners found themselves in the midst of a flurry of blue flashing lights and policemen in heavy boots. Grace kept thinking to herself, 'Mind my carpet!', the most irrational of thoughts considering the grave circumstances, but nevertheless this was not a time to think sanely.

"Dick Thomas, I am arresting you. . . ." Alf Harrison was saying, waving his police identity card, "You do not have to say anything. . . "

Grace was in a fuzzy bubble, unable to comprehend that the events unfolding in her pristine kitchen were actually going to affect her. Dick looked shocked and aged. Grace felt her own hands being cuffed behind her back, and watched as the two detectives carried out their duties, the uniformed officers now having gone to the sitting room to gather the guests together. Of course, she realised, Alf and Eric were no more brothers than Dick was faithful. And then it came to her, the notion that would save Grace's bacon.

"It'll be alright love," Dick was calling to her, "Don't worry."

Grace smiled, the same faint humour playing on her lips that had presented itself a few days before. She didn't feel in the least perturbed by the look of anguish on his face.

"I know," she mouthed to her husband.

Dick frowned, not quite understanding what his wife meant, so she happily enlightened him.

"I know about you and Sheila Collins."

At the police station, some hours later, sitting in an interview room with a lukewarm cup of tea in front of her, Grace allowed the tears to roll freely down her cheeks.

"I'm very sorry that we had to bring you here under caution Mrs. Thomas," Alf Harrison was saying as he entered the room, "We can see that you had no part in all this."

"I see," Grace sighed, "All what exactly?"

"We already have a confession from your husband. He has freely admitted to killing Mr. Brown, Mr. Wellings and Mr. Lewis," Eric Harrison was telling her calmly, "We just need a few details from you and then you can be released. I know this must be such a shock for you Grace, is there anyone we can call?"

She shook her head and continued to look at the grey stone floor under her feet, "No, it's fine."

"Of course, you'll need to stay with someone for a while," the detective continued, "We need to erm, search the house and dig up the patio."

"The patio?" Grace quizzed, furrowing her brow.

"He says that's where he put the bodies," the policeman explained awkwardly, wondering how to avoid causing this very plain little woman any more distress than was really necessary.

In a moment of realisation, Grace formed an 'O' with her mouth and waited for the man to continue.

"Best if you're not around," he said, tapping the table top with his fingers, "It won't be easy."

Grace nodded. She could go to her parents until after Dick's trial.

"How did you know?" she whispered softly, looking intently at the man in front of her.

"Your husband wrote it all down in the back of that Quentin Crisp poetry book," Detective Harrison explained, "Names, dates, times and even how much money he'd stolen from them."

Grace shuddered, suddenly feeling the draught from an open window.

"What about the guests!" she exclaimed, panicking about the families who ought to be waiting for their evening meal.

"They've all gone home," Alf Harrison sighed, digging his hands deep into the pockets of his dark trousers, "The Sandybank is closed until further notice Grace."

In another interview room Dick Thomas was putting a signature to the last page of his statement.

"You'll be held in custody at Winchmere until a date is set for your trial," a burly policeman was telling him, "Do you understand Dick?"

The hotel proprietor nodded, "My wife?" he asked tearfully.

"Sorry pal," another uniformed officer told him, "She's refusing to see you, and you can hardly blame her in the circumstances can you?"

Dick felt in his trouser pocket and pulled out the single cigarette that he kept for stressful situations.

"Alright if I smoke this before we go?" he asked.

The policeman gave his consent and offered the prisoner a light.

Before he had smoked the Woodbine to the end, Dick felt his chest constrict tightly and he fell to his knees, involuntarily foaming at the mouth and choking on his own vomit as he went.

The officers dashed across the room to save their prisoner, both having the same thought, that Dick Thomas had died from a heart attack, shocked, as the terror of what he'd done dawned on him.

Six Months Later

As Grace sat sipping a strong black coffee on the balcony of her hotel, she reflected upon the events of the last twelve months. Now a couple of stone lighter thanks to a Mediterranean diet, and her thick curly hair dyed a deep auburn, she was a changed woman, a stronger woman.

If she was honest with herself, Grace was happier and more determined than she had ever been in her marriage to Dick. If only he hadn't cheated, things might have turned out much differently, she thought, maybe they could have started afresh in another seaside town, and maybe their love for each other could have been rekindled. But no, Grace reminded herself, nothing would be the same after Sheila Collins.

Looking out to sea, with a mild westward wind ruffling her curls, Grace took another sip of her drink and cast her eyes down towards the village below. The local Italian villagers were rushing off to church, the older women dressed in black and the men smartly striding along in their best suits. What were they going to confess, Grace asked herself. Had these simple foreign people any real sins that required God's forgiveness? She doubted very much that there would be anything to disclose.

"Unlike me," she murmured aloud, "God would send a lightning bolt if he only knew."

It had all started the afternoon before Mr. Brown's departure from the Sandybank. Grace had gone upstairs to put fresh soap and a pitcher of water on his bedside table and noticed a small brown box sticking out from underneath the bed. Mr. Brown was on one of his long walks at the time and, as he was very predictable in his movements, Grace knew that he wouldn't be back until just before dinner. She had stood for a few moments just looking at the hard metal exterior of the box, deciding whether she could resist temptation, a few moments contemplation proved that she could not.

Carefully sliding the object out from its hiding place, Grace could see that this was an old-fashioned money tin. Her own grandfather had kept his savings in a similar container, high out of reach atop a Welsh dresser. It was obvious to Grace that Mr. Brown felt it safer to carry his money around with him, rather than leave it at home. As she lifted the lid, Grace Thomas gasped. She had never seen such a vast amount of cash and it caused saliva to fill her mouth. She also felt a huge pang of animosity towards Mr. Brown. Here was an elderly gent, with no family and no obvious signs of extravagance in his clothing or tastes, hoarding more money than he could spend in his lifetime. Grace was quick to remind herself that this particular guest had never so much as left a tip when he had departed on previous holidays, counting out his board money in dribs and drabs as if he were frightened to leave sixpence too much.

Grace touched the notes on the top of the pile, imagining how life-changing this amount could be for her and Dick. In a split decision, she knew what she had to do.

At first she had intended administering the poison at breakfast the next morning. Mr. Brown was so set upon his bowl of porridge topped with cold milk and brown sugar that it would come almost as second nature to Grace, to stir in the rat poison. Then the silly old man had asked for that extra hour, upsetting her plans and causing Grace to think quickly. At first, it had been difficult to persuade Dick to go along with her plan, but after threatening to leave him, Grace had eventually found herself a willing partner in crime. Dick insisted that he would play no part in killing Mr. Brown he said, but admitted that it wouldn't be too much of a hardship to put him under the patio afterwards. So, in a moment of genius, Grace had set out the tea things, tipped rat poison into the pot leaving Dick to do one small task, which was simply to convince Mr. Brown to take refreshments before what he thought would be a long journey home. In reality death had been swift and the furthest their guest had to travel was actually just Dick dragging him by the legs to a deep hole in the garden.

Josiah Wellings had been far too flash for Grace's liking and carried his cash around with him in his pockets. Therefore his downfall had been convincing Dick to have a farewell drink with him on the morning of his departure. They had returned to the potting shed just before noon, where the remnants of the cherry brandy sat upon the shelf, alongside Dick's tools and homemade cider. Grace had predicted that the two men would toast their friendship in this way and had laced the drink with more from her bottle of poison. She had warned Dick not to touch it and, within the hour, as Dick opened his second can of beer, Josiah Wellings began to foam at the mouth in the first of his torturous convulsions. It had been easy for Dick to close the potting shed door until death had claimed their guest, and thirty minutes later he was pulling Mr. Wellings little body across the lawn to a damp and earthy grave. Grace wrinkled her nose as she recalled listening to Josiah Wellings' nasal voice. What an annoying little man he had been. She had been peeved at finding only a small amount of cash amongst his belongings, and the fake banknotes had had to be destroyed on a bonfire.

Lastly, had been the very affluent Mr. Lewis. Oh how Grace Thomas loved the way that these old men trusted no-one and carried their life savings around with them!

Grace had planned to lace Mr. Lewis's fish pie with toxins the night before his departure, but then realised that they needed all of their guests to sign the register on the morning that they left, just in case anyone ever came looking. Therefore, after a rethink, she had fixed upon the idea of mixing it into the elderly man's scrambled eggs. When

Dick had told her of Mr. Lewis's early exit, Grace had been too delighted at finding the huge quantity of notes to ask how their guest had met his end. She was also genuinely delighted that the patio was finished and their nest egg full.

Everything had gone according to plan, although not exactly like clockwork, the Thomas's had achieved their goal. They had been very careful to act as though they genuinely had no idea where the three missing men had gone, just in case other guests had overheard, and had carried on their lives with no hint of alteration. And so life would have continued, until their grand voyage to sunnier climes, if it hadn't been for Sheila Collins.

Grace shifted slightly in her seat and reflected about the ones that got away. Lovely Henry Patterson had been the instigation behind Dick smartening himself up, and the couple had jointly agreed that they needed reasonable time between killings, in order to keep suspicion at bay. There was Mr. Baxter too, but finding nothing of any value amongst his possessions, Dick had convinced his wife that it would be pointless digging another hole just for the sake of it.

Her coffee was going slightly cold by now, and Grace swirled around the dregs as she thought about that dark Ford Anglia car. She wished dearly that she'd taken more notice of it, hardly expecting to be under full police surveillance but in the end it hadn't mattered. She smiled her infamous wry smile, fancy Dick writing everything down in that silly little book, she thought, even the sums of money that Oscar had given him were noted down in there, although she never did find out the reason for it.

Grace hadn't wanted to kill Dick. She loved him, a kind of soulmate for twenty years, he had been reliable, stable and unchanging, everything that she had wanted in a husband. But once the seed of suspicion had been planted, there was no way could she forgive him. It might only have been one night of senseless passion with her best friend, but Grace could never forget. It had been the night before they were to be betrothed, when she had been sitting in the living room with her mother listening to endless advice and having her curls wrapped tightly in rags for her wedding day.

On the morning that Grace had left to book her flight to Italy, she had carefully mashed up boiled eggs with salad cream and some of the poison. It hadn't been enough to kill her husband, just enough to warn him and give him stomach cramps. The final dose had been administered when she had slipped a Woodbine into Dick's trouser pocket on the day of his arrest. That had been a genius move on Grace's part. She had always known about Dick's secret smoking habit when he was nervous or stressed, so that morning, as he washed in the bathroom, she had taken his emergency cigarette down to the kitchen and dipped the filter in rat poison. Dick wouldn't notice until he needed to smoke, she had thought at the time, and that wouldn't be until she had revealed her plans to leave him. As soon as Sheila Collins's name had left her lips on that fateful afternoon, she knew that Dick would be so eaten up with guilt that two things would happen. Firstly, he would swear that Grace was completely innocent, merely a pawn caught up in her husband's devious games. Secondly, Dick would be so stressed that he would need that final cigarette.

Grace turned to look through the French doors as a deep voice beckoned.

"Come back to bed, it's far too early to get up."

She smiled and put down her coffee cup, admiring the strong muscular curves of Robbie Powell's body as he lay eyeing her seductively from underneath cream silk sheets.

"I want to make the most of every single day," she told him, "You never know what might happen."